MW01063099

28944

PORTRAITS
of LITTLE WOMEN

Christmas
Dreams

Don't miss any of the
Portraits of Little Women

PORTRAITS
of LITTLE WOMEN

*Christmas
Dreams*

Four Stories

Susan Beth Pfeffer

DELACORTE PRESS

Published by
Delacorte Press
Bantam Doubleday Dell Publishing Group, Inc.
1540 Broadway
New York, New York 10036

Library of Congress Cataloging-in-Publication Data
Pfeffer, Susan Beth.
    Portraits of Little women. Christmas dreams : four stories / Susan
Beth Pfeffer.
        p.   cm.
    Summary: As each of the four March sisters turns ten, she is invited
by Aunt March at Christmastime to discuss who will receive an heirloom,
an old cameo brooch, and thus each girl contemplates her role in the
family.
    ISBN 0-385-32623-8
    [1. Christmas—Fiction.   2. Sisters—Fiction.   3. Aunts—Fiction.
4. Family life—New England—Fiction.   5. New England—Fiction.]
    I. Title.
PZ7.P44855P1f   1998
[Fic]—dc21
                                                                    98-19845
                                                                        CIP
                                                                         AC

The text of this book is set in 13-point Cochin.

Book design by Patrice Sheridan
Cover illustration copyright © 1998 by Lori Earley
Text and craft illustrations copyright © 1998 by Marcy Ramsey
Recipe illustrations copyright © 1998 by Laura Maestro

Manufactured in the United States of America

November 1998

10   9   8   7   6   5   4   3   2

BVG

HOLIDAY WISHES
TO ALL MY READERS

CONTENTS

Meg's Christmas Dream

Marmee says when she was a girl she used to write letters to herself, with the intention of reading them when she was all grown up. I always thought that was a nice idea, but I've never done it. This Christmas I've decided to. I don't know why now, but maybe it's because I'm ten and I won't be a child much longer.

We are very happy this Christmas. We're all in good health. Father is busy year-round, but, of course, being a minister, he has even more to do at Christmas. And Marmee keeps busy taking care of all of us, in addition to doing her charity work.

As for my younger sisters, Jo has been working on a play for us to perform. Beth practices the piano and has learned many new songs. And Amy follows all of us around, wanting to draw our pictures.

Hannah, who has been our faithful housekeeper for as long as I can remember, plans to prepare a fine Christmas feast. She works so hard and is loved by us all. Marmee doesn't know how she could manage without her.

This is an especially exciting Christmas season because I paid a visit to Aunt March the other day. She showed me a cameo brooch her husband, Uncle March, had given to her. It had belonged to his mother, who was Father's grandmother.

Aunt March said she'd been waiting for one of us to be old enough to give it to, and now that I was ten, she thought perhaps the time had come. But she wasn't certain whether I should have it, or Jo, or Beth, or Amy when they reach my age. I promised not to mention the brooch to them, since Aunt March isn't certain which one of us is the proper March girl to inherit such a family treasure.

I should dearly love to own the brooch. Cameos are the most beautiful kind of jewelry, and it would be so special to have something that belonged to Father's grandmother. She died when he was just a boy, but he remembers her as a beautiful and gentle lady.

I hope when I grow up I shall be a beautiful and gentle lady as well. Perhaps if Aunt March were to give me the cameo, I could use it as a reminder of all I want to be.

Meg March

CHAPTER 1

"Oh, look," said Meg March as she and Jo walked through the town of Concord on a brisk December afternoon. "A book dealer has just opened a shop." She stopped to look at the plaque above the door. " 'William Marshall, Book Dealer,' " she read aloud.

Jo pressed her nose against the window. "I've never seen so many books," she said. "Except perhaps in Mr. Emerson's library."

"Not even Mr. Emerson has that many books," Meg replied, thinking of their wealthy neighbor's impressive library. "Wouldn't it be splendid, Jo, to walk into such a shop and buy whichever books you desired?"

"Christopher Columbus," Jo said. "Splendid beyond belief."

"Don't use slang," Meg scolded. "You know it isn't proper for a lady."

"But I'm not a lady," Jo protested. "I'm a nine-year-old girl. And I say you and I should go into the shop and look at the books even if we can't buy any."

Meg frowned. "I don't know. Do you think we ought to?"

"I'm going to be a writer someday," Jo said. "It's important for me to see what sorts of books get published."

Meg had no writing ambitions, but she followed her younger sister into the shop.

"This isn't a place for children," the bookseller said as Jo and Meg walked in. "We have no books that would be of interest to you."

"How do you know what sorts of books interest us?" Jo asked.

The bookseller eyed her suspiciously. "How old are you?" he asked. He looked about Father's age, but he certainly didn't have Father's sweet, friendly face.

"Nine," Jo said.

"Just as I thought. You're too young. Come

8

back next year," the bookseller said. "Only people ten years of age and older find our books of interest."

"But my sister—" Before Jo had a chance to complete her sentence, Meg grabbed her and pushed her out the door.

"You could have stayed," Jo said as they stood outside. "You're ten."

"I'll come some other time," Meg said. She edged her way around a snowbank to get a better view of the store's window. "Oh, Jo, look at that beautiful Bible."

Jo came closer. "It is lovely," she agreed. The Bible was open to a map of the Holy Land. "I'll go there someday. After I've been to Europe, but before I go to China."

"What a perfect Christmas present that would make for Father," said Meg. "It's so much larger than our family Bible. And it has a map."

"Actually, it has many," Jo said. " 'Maps of the Holy Land, Jerusalem, and Other Biblical Locations,' " she said, reading a sign next to the open book.

"Father would treasure such a gift," Meg said. "He could look up locations on the

9

maps and tell people about them in his sermons."

"Father certainly deserves such a Bible," Jo agreed. "I wonder how much it costs."

"A great deal of money, I'm sure," Meg said. "It's so beautiful. And if it weren't expensive, the book dealer would surely advertise its price."

"That's clever of you," Jo said. "I'm going back to ask what it costs. Then we can tell Father about it."

"No, I'll go in," Meg said. "I'm ten, after all." She smiled at Jo and reentered the comfortably warm store.

"You've returned," the book dealer said. "I told you I have nothing of interest to children."

"But I'm ten years old," Meg said. "And you said your books were of interest to people ten years old and older."

"I assumed you were nine too," the book dealer said. "Are you sure you're ten?"

"Quite sure," Meg replied. "Are you Mr. William Marshall?"

"Yes, I am. Why do you ask?"

"If you're Mr. Marshall, then you must

know how much the Bible costs," said Meg. "The beautiful one in the window with the maps of the Holy Land."

"It costs far more than you can afford," Mr. Marshall said. "How much money do you have?"

Meg thought about it. She had two dollars saved up to buy cloth for a new dress. And with Christmas coming, Aunt March might well give her a dollar. "Three dollars," she said.

"I thought as much," Mr. Marshall said. "That's why children aren't allowed in this shop. The Bible you admire costs ten dollars."

"Ten dollars!" Meg cried. "For a book?"

"A holy book," Mr. Marshall said. "With maps. It's well worth it."

"I should so like to buy it for my father," Meg said. "He's the Reverend March, a minister. Of course he has a Bible, but not nearly as beautiful a one as that. And the maps would be so useful for him."

"The price is still ten dollars," Mr. Marshall said. "If your father has that much to spend, then he can come himself, and I'll be pleased to sell it to him."

"I don't think he has ten dollars," Meg said. "We don't have very much money. Aunt March says we're poor as church mice."

"Does this aunt March of yours have financial means?" Mr. Marshall asked.

"Oh, yes," Meg said. "Although we're not supposed to notice."

"Then ask her to buy the Bible for your father," Mr. Marshall suggested.

"Aunt March doesn't like to buy Father presents," Meg said. "She believes there's no point in giving fine things to a man who thinks only of Heaven and its rewards."

Mr. Marshall shook his head. "Come back when you're eleven. Perhaps then you'll be able to afford it."

Meg doubted she would. "Thank you anyway," she said, and left the store.

"How much does it cost?" Jo asked as she linked an arm with Meg's for warmth.

"Ten dollars," Meg said.

"Christopher Columbus!" said Jo.

Meg nodded. "Christopher Columbus indeed."

CHAPTER 2

"It isn't fair," Amy said.

"What isn't?" Meg asked. She was sitting in the room she shared with Jo. Amy and Beth were sprawled on Jo's bed.

"That we don't have any money," Amy replied. "Other girls have money, and they're not nearly as nice as we."

"Niceness doesn't have anything to do with it," Jo said. "Otherwise Aunt March would be a pauper and Father and Marmee would be rich as kings."

"We're as happy as kings," Beth pointed out. "Aren't we, Jo?"

"I'm not so sure kings are happy," Jo said. "They aren't in the stories I read."

"If I were rich, I'd be terribly happy," Amy

declared. "You might not care about money, Beth, but I do."

Jo laughed. "What do you know about money?" she asked. "You're only six, still a baby."

"I know we don't have any, and Aunt March has more than she'll ever need," Amy said. "And I'm not a baby."

"Amy's right," Meg said. "Aunt March has a great deal of wealth, and we don't have nearly enough."

"We have enough to eat and keep warm," Beth said. "There are people with less than that."

"I know," Meg said. "And truly, I count our blessings. But I would so love to give Father that Bible for Christmas." She sighed. "I don't think I'll ever see ten dollars in my life."

"I wish you could," Jo said. "Mr. Marshall was so rude to us, Meg, and I'd so like for you to be able to throw ten dollars at him and walk off with that Bible."

"I'd like that too," Meg said. "Mr. Marshall acted as though I didn't deserve to be in his precious shop."

"But how can you get ten dollars?" Beth

15

asked. "I'll give you all I have, Meg, but it's only fifty cents."

"I don't even have that," Jo said. "I'm afraid I spent all my money on pens and paper last week."

"And I don't have any money," Amy said. "I'm just a baby."

"Aunt March might give us money for Christmas," Jo said. "She did last year. If she gives us each a dollar and we give them to you for the Bible, how much money will you have?"

"Four dollars from Aunt March and my own two dollars," Meg said.

"And my fifty cents," Beth said.

"Six dollars and fifty cents," Meg said. "Still short of ten."

Jo sighed. "Then Father will never have that Bible. And Mr. Marshall will never have to treat you with respect."

"There must be a way," Meg said, but she couldn't imagine what it might be.

That night Meg went to bed thinking of nothing but the Bible. The more she thought about it, the more beautiful it became. She tried not to feel angry, but it was hard not to.

It wasn't as though she wanted money for herself. It was for Father. In years past, she had handmade Father's Christmas presents, but now that she was ten, she felt it was time to give him something store-bought.

All these thoughts and feelings swirled in her head, and it took her a long time to fall asleep. When she did, she dreamed she was at Aunt March's. Only, as rich as Aunt March's house usually was, in Meg's dream, everything there was made of gold.

"Aunt March," Meg said, looking about her in awe. "I never knew you were so wealthy. You're as rich as a king."

"You're not supposed to notice," Aunt March said. "But yes, I am rich, Margaret. I am the richest person on earth."

"I should like to have ten dollars," Meg said. "For Father. He thinks of Heaven, so he has no money."

"In Heaven there is no need for money," Aunt March reasoned. "Although when I go to Heaven, I shall continue to be rich."

"Might I have ten dollars?" Meg asked.

"No," Aunt March said. "But I'll give you all my jewelry instead. Would you like that,

Margaret? I have emeralds and rubies, and they will be yours."

"Mine?" Meg asked.

Suddenly Aunt March was covered in gleaming jewels. "All yours," she declared. She removed a diamond tiara and tossed it into the air. "All these jewels belonged to your great-grandmother. Your father doesn't have any because all he thinks about is Heaven. But they're yours, Margaret, if only you ask for them."

"Please, Aunt March, please," Meg said, reaching out and trying to grab the jewelry. But Aunt March moved farther and farther away, laughing at Meg and throwing ornate bracelets and necklaces out the window.

Meg woke up shaking. Aunt March wasn't the richest person in the world. And she didn't have diamonds and emeralds, at least none that Meg knew about. But Aunt March did have a cameo that she was thinking of giving to Meg. And if Meg could be its new owner, then she might be able to trade it for a Bible.

CHAPTER 3

"Go on home without me," Meg said to Jo the next day after school. "I'm going to visit Aunt March."

"And ask her for ten dollars?" Jo said. "Do you think she'll give it to you?"

"I have another idea," Meg said. She longed to tell Jo about the brooch, but Aunt March had made her promise not to.

"Well," Jo said, "what is it?"

"I'll tell you only if it works," Meg said. "Do wish me luck, Jo."

"You'll need more than luck to ask a favor of Aunt March," Jo said. "You'll need the courage of a lion. Are you sure you don't want me to go with you? Aunt March doesn't frighten me."

"I'll be fine," Meg said. "And perhaps when I return, I'll have a way to purchase the Bible."

"I'll tell Marmee where you are," Jo said. "And I do wish you well, Meg."

Meg smiled and watched as Jo turned to go home. Aunt March's house was a bit farther away from town, and as Meg continued her journey, she carefully avoided patches of ice, all the while thinking of how frightening Aunt March was, especially when you wanted something from her. But beneath all her bluster, Meg knew Aunt March had a good heart. Or so Marmee said, and Marmee never lied.

Meg knocked on the wreath-decorated door, and Williams, Aunt March's butler, appeared. "Good afternoon, Miss Margaret," he said. "Is your aunt expecting you?"

"I don't think so," Meg said. "Might I come in anyway?"

"Of course," Williams said.

Meg was glad to get out of the cold. She could see a fire burning in the back parlor and longed to stand in front of it.

"I'll tell Mrs. March you're here," Williams said.

Meg thanked him. She looked around at Aunt March's many possessions. Any one thing—a silver bowl, a Gilbert Stuart painting, or a crystal chandelier—could purchase a thousand Bibles, she was sure. Amy was right. It really wasn't fair.

"Your aunt will see you now," Williams told Meg. She followed him into the back parlor, where Aunt March was keeping warm sitting by the fire.

Meg curtsied and Aunt March indicated that she should kiss her, which Meg did.

"This is a pleasant surprise," Aunt March declared. "I trust all is well with you and your family, Margaret."

"Oh, yes, Aunt March," Meg said.

"And you simply decided to pay a call on your lonely old aunt," Aunt March said. "You're here to extend Christmas greetings to me, no doubt?"

"Oh, yes," Meg said. "Have a very merry Christmas, Aunt March."

"I suppose you're also here to find out what I intend to give you," Aunt March said. "Children your age are always curious about such things."

"I was wondering about the cameo," Meg admitted. She felt her face turn red and knew it wasn't from the warmth cast by the fire. "I was wondering if I might be getting it."

"I haven't yet decided," Aunt March said. "Or are you here to tell me why you should be the one I give it to?"

"Well, yes," Meg said. "I suppose that is why I'm here." She wished Aunt March would tell her to sit. It only made her more uncomfortable to be standing. Meg had never noticed before how much Aunt March's chair resembled a throne.

"Very well," Aunt March said. "You may begin, Margaret. Why do you deserve to be given the cameo?"

"It isn't so much that I deserve it," Meg said. "I'm sure Jo is every bit as deserving as I am, or Beth, or Amy. Although I am the oldest, and I suppose that counts for something."

"Will you care for it better because you are the oldest?" Aunt March asked. "Do you think you're more trustworthy than your sisters?"

"Jo does make a mess of things," Meg said. "But Beth is quite tidy. And Amy cherishes her belongings so much, I'm sure she would care for the cameo should you give it to her. But that's not why you should give it to me anyway. Assuming you want to give it to me, that is."

"Tell me then," said Aunt March. "Why should you be so honored?"

"Because I need it the most," Meg said. "Not for me, Aunt March. For Father."

"Your father needs a brooch?" Aunt March asked. "I've never known him to wear one."

Meg suspected this was Aunt March's attempt at humor, but in case it wasn't, she didn't laugh, only smiled. "Not to wear, Aunt March," she said. "Actually, I don't mean to tell him about the cameo at all."

"Then why does he need it? What is the point of this mystery, Margaret?"

"Father is the best man in the world," Meg said. "I'm sure you know that, Aunt March. He never asks for anything for himself. He gives all he can to Marmee and to me and my sisters, and whatever might be left, he gives to those in need. And so this year, I should so like to give him a Christmas present worthy of him. Something store-bought and fine."

"And what might that present be?" Aunt March asked.

"A Bible," Meg said. "Oh, Aunt March, I know exactly the one I want and it is so beautiful. It has maps of all the places mentioned in the text. Jo saw it too and agreed it's the loveliest Bible ever." Meg paused. "But it costs ten dollars," she went on. "Jo, Amy, Beth, and I added up what each of us had, but we didn't have anything close to that amount."

"And what does this have to do with the cameo?" Aunt March asked.

Meg took a deep breath. "I thought perhaps if you gave me the cameo, as you said you might, I could sell it and get the ten dollars for the Bible."

"You planned to *sell* the cameo?" Aunt March said, leaning forward. "A brooch that has been in the March family for four generations?"

Meg looked down at the floor and wished it would open up and swallow her whole. "Father deserves a fine Bible," she mumbled.

"Your father deserves a daughter with a little bit of sense," Aunt March said. "One who does not throw away a family heirloom on a whim."

"It's not a whim," Meg said. "I've been thinking about it since last night."

"Since last night," Aunt March echoed. "Forgive me. I didn't realize so much of your life had been devoted to this foolish idea."

"It didn't seem like such a foolish idea when I thought of it," Meg said. "I'd sell another of my possessions, Aunt March, if I owned anything valuable."

"Well, if you continue to have such foolish and wasteful ideas, you never will," Aunt March said. "I am very disappointed in you, Margaret. I seriously thought of giving you the cameo. I thought you were a responsible girl who would be worthy of owning such an heirloom. I even thought you'd be glad to pass it on to your own daughter when she was old enough to be given it. Now I can see I was wrong. You are far too much like your father. Generosity is a virtue, but not to excess. Family heirlooms are not meant to be tossed aside. I shall not give you the cameo, Margaret. I'm not sure I'll ever give you a Christmas present again. You may now leave."

"Yes, Aunt March," Meg said. She longed to ask Aunt March if that meant there'd be no gift of money either, but she didn't dare. Instead she curtsied in farewell and left Aunt March's house of splendor to return to her own humble home.

CHAPTER 4

"Tell me, daughters," Father said at supper that night. "Did you have good days today?"

"I thought all about Christmas," Amy replied. "Did you know Mr. Emerson has a Christmas tree?"

"Yes, he told me he was getting one," Father said. "We must go over and admire it. What else did you girls do?"

"Beth was a special help to Hannah today," Marmee said. "She peeled the potatoes we're eating this evening."

"And well peeled they are," Father said. "Thank you, Beth."

"You're welcome," Beth said. "I like helping

with the housework. I'd much rather do that than go to school."

"I wouldn't," Jo said. "I know it's necessary to do housework, but school is more important. Isn't it, Father?"

"All work is important," Father said, "as long as it's productive and helps others."

"How does going to school help others?" Amy asked.

"That's a very good question," Father said. "Meg, do you know the answer?"

"Pardon?" Meg asked. She'd been thinking about the Bible and how good it would look in Father's library.

"Meg has her mind on other things," Marmee said. "Tell us, Meg, how was your visit with Aunt March?"

Meg didn't know how to answer. The chance existed that Aunt March would tell Father and Marmee of her visit. But Meg had also been told not to mention the cameo to her sisters. "It was all right," she said.

"I'm sure Aunt March was pleased to see you," Marmee said. "Why did you choose today for a visit?"

Meg put down her fork and tried to work

out an answer. "I had something to ask her," she said. "I saw a present I wanted to purchase for you, Father, for Christmas, only I don't have the money. I thought perhaps Aunt March might help me. But of course she isn't going to."

"You asked her for money?" Father asked.

"Not exactly," Meg said. "I asked her for something she'd said she might give me. Only she got angry and said I couldn't have it, so now I'll never have the money I need for your present. I'm sorry, Father. I wanted you to have it so much. Jo saw it too, didn't you, Jo?"

"Yes," Jo said. "It would have been just perfect for you, Father."

Father smiled. "I appreciate your thinking of me," he said. "But I have all I need sitting at this table with me: a loving wife and four healthy daughters. What greater gift could I wish for?"

"But you deserve more," Meg said. "I wanted to give you something special for Christmas this year. I'm ten now, and not a little girl, and I just knew you'd like it."

"I'm sure if it came from you, I'd like it a

29

great deal, whatever it is," Father said. "But Meg, I don't need expensive gifts. Last year you knitted me a scarf, and I wear it still. And each time I put it on, I think of you and the effort you took, and I cherish it all the more."

"Handmade gifts are the nicest," Marmee said. "I love the gifts you girls make far more than I would care for anything from a store."

"Was Aunt March angry with you when you left?" Father asked.

Meg nodded.

"Then you would be wise to send her a note of apology," he said. "Aunt March can be difficult, but I'm sure she thinks she was right to turn you down. And since I don't know exactly what you asked of her, it's possible that she is right. What do you think now that you've had some time to consider it, Meg?"

"She might have been right," Meg said. She thought about the cameo and the fact that Aunt March had never truly promised it to her. What if she had decided to give it to Jo or Beth or Amy instead? Then Meg would have deprived her sister of the chance to own a family heirloom that she could give to her own daughter someday. Although it was hard to imagine Jo or Beth or Amy ever being old enough to have a daughter. In spite of herself, Meg smiled.

"What do you find so funny?" Jo asked. "Surely it can't be Aunt March."

"No," Meg said. "Father, how long will it take before we are grown up?"

Father smiled back. "It will happen sooner than you can imagine," he said. "Far sooner than I care to think."

Meg looked at her younger sisters and still thought it impossible that they could ever all be grown up. Her sisters must have shared the thought, for before Meg knew it, they had joined her in laughter.

CHAPTER 5

"Do you still have that fifty cents?" Meg asked Beth Saturday afternoon. She stood in the doorway of Beth's bedroom. Beth was dressing one of her dolls. Amy was there also, brushing her hair.

"Yes," Beth said. "Why, Meg?"

"I've decided to go back to Mr. Marshall's," Meg said. "Maybe if I give him your fifty cents and my two dollars, he'll change his mind and let me have the Bible."

"Do you really think so?" Beth asked. "He sounds awfully mean."

"I'm not sure," Meg said. "But I have nothing to lose by asking. And Aunt March might still give you and Jo and Amy money for Christmas, and then I could add that to the two dollars and fifty cents. And perhaps I could work for the rest. I'll only know if I ask him."

"Here's my fifty cents, then," Beth said.

"I have twenty-five cents," Amy admitted. "I was saving it for hair ribbons, but if you think it would help, I'll let you have it."

"Thank you," Meg said. "If I can purchase the Bible, I'll be sure to tell Father it's from all of us."

"All of us except Jo," Amy said. "She hasn't given any money."

"I'm sure she will when she has some," Meg said. "Now I have two dollars and seventy-five cents. Perhaps that will be enough for Mr. Marshall."

"Shall I go with you?" Amy asked. "If I tell Mr. Marshall how I gave up new hair ribbons, maybe he'll be more willing to sell you the Bible."

"Thank you, but I don't think so," Meg said. "He doesn't like anyone under the age of ten in his store."

"Then I won't come either," Beth said. Meg smiled. Beth was terribly shy and hated meeting new people. But Meg knew that if Beth had thought it would make a difference, she would have come.

"I have to do this alone," Meg said. "Not even Jo can help."

Deep down, Meg wished her sisters were coming along for support. She suspected Mr. Marshall wouldn't be very welcoming. But she had to take the chance. She took the money and put it in her purse. It was more money than she'd ever held at one time, and it made her even more nervous that much of it wasn't hers.

She clutched the purse to her side as she walked under the gentle snowfall. Meg loved Concord at this time of year. People she knew greeted her along the way. Many were carrying packages, no doubt Christmas presents for loved ones or food for Christmas dinners. Everyone was happy and smiling.

This helped Meg be more positive about her errand, but she paused when she reached the bookstore. First she checked the window. The Bible was still there. At ten dollars, she supposed few people in Concord could afford it, except perhaps Aunt March.

She looked into the shop and saw that Mr.

Marshall was busy with customers. She waited until they had left. Then she walked in.

"It's you," Mr. Marshall said. "Are you still ten?"

"Yes, sir," Meg replied. "I won't be eleven for quite a while yet."

"I thought perhaps you were nine again," Mr. Marshall said. "But I suppose you're determined to be ten."

"For the time being," Meg said. She smiled in case Mr. Marshall was joking. She wished people like Mr. Marshall and Aunt March would announce when they were making jokes, so that she'd know better when to laugh.

"Have you decided to make a purchase?" Mr. Marshall asked.

"I still want your Bible," Meg said. "The beautiful one in the window. I've brought some money."

"How much?" Mr. Marshall asked.

"Two dollars and seventy-five cents," Meg said. "It's all the money my sisters and I have. My little sister Amy gave me twenty-five cents that she'd been saving for hair ribbons. She has lovely blond curls. And my sister Beth

gave me fifty cents. She would have come with me today, even though she's terribly shy."

"Which sister did I see you with the other day?" Mr. Marshall asked. "I didn't notice blond curls, and she certainly didn't seem shy."

"That was Jo," Meg said. "She wants to be a writer. Someday you might sell her books in your store. She would have given me her money, but she doesn't have any. Someday she will, though, and she'll give it to me, because we'd all like Father to have that Bible."

"And I'd like it if you had the ten dollars," Mr. Marshall said. "But I have to sell my books at a fair price if I'm to stay in business. I can't just give them away."

"I know," Meg said. "I thought perhaps I could convince you to let me have the Bible if I told you I'd pay you the rest of the money when I got it."

"And when might that be?" Mr. Marshall asked.

"I don't know," Meg admitted. "But I'd work and save, and so would my sisters. Aunt March will surely give them some money at Christmas. She's angry with me, though, for saying I'd take the cameo she said she might give me and sell it for money for the Bible. But I'd work hard to earn what I owe you. Do you think there's any chance you could sell me the Bible? Christmas is just two days away, and I would love for Father to have it."

"No," Mr. Marshall said. "There isn't any chance at all."

"I'm sorry," Meg said.

"You know something?" Mr. Marshall said. "I'm sorry too."

CHAPTER 6

"I still think he should have sold it to you," Jo said as the girls sat in Meg's room.

"So do I," Amy said. "Especially when you told him about the hair ribbons."

"I suppose it's because he doesn't know Father," Beth said. "If he did, he'd realize what a fine man he is and how much he'd appreciate such a splendid book."

"I've done all I can," Meg said. "I just hope I haven't spoiled Christmas for everyone."

"My Christmas isn't spoiled," Amy said. "For now I have the money for hair ribbons."

The girls laughed.

"Girls! It's time for supper!" Marmee called.

Meg and her sisters ran down the stairs. A bright fire was burning in the parlor, and the supper table had been set. Father and Marmee were already seated, and Hannah was just finishing putting out the food.

Father said the blessing, and they all began to eat. It was a simple meal, nothing like the Christmas dinner they'd be sharing in two days. As Meg thought about the dinner and what gift she could possibly make for Father in time for Christmas, someone knocked on the front door.

"I wonder who that could be," Father said.

"No one in trouble, I hope," Marmee said.

Meg stood up. "I'll get it," she said. Father and Marmee had worked all day, and she knew they were tired. She went to the door. To her dismay, Mr. Marshall was standing there.

"I see I'm at the right house," he said. "Good evening, Miss March."

"Mr. Marshall," Meg said. "Would you like to come in?"

"Yes, thank you."

"Meg, who is it?" Father called from the

parlor. "Bring our company in, whoever it might be."

"Please come this way," Meg said to Mr. Marshall. She led him the few feet into the parlor.

"Welcome, sir," Father said, getting up from the table. "Warm yourself by our fire. Can I offer you some supper? Nothing fancy, but warm and filling."

"Thank you, sir, but I'll have something at home. I came to see your daughter Meg," Mr. Marshall said. "My name is William Marshall."

"The bookseller?" Father asked, and his face lit up with pleasure. "Please do join us, sir. Mr. Emerson has spoken of nothing but your store since it opened. I look forward to visiting it myself when Christmas is over and I have more time."

"Hannah, there'll be one more for supper," Marmee said. "Jo, be a dear and get a chair for Mr. Marshall. Meg, tell us how you happen to know each other."

"It was at Mr. Marshall's store that I saw the gift I wanted for Father," Meg said. "The one that costs too much money."

"That's why I've come," Mr. Marshall said. He looked at Father and Marmee. "Would you mind if I spoke to Meg privately for a bit?" he asked them.

"Not at all. Why don't you take Mr. Marshall into the kitchen, Meg?" said Father.

Meg didn't know what the bookseller could possibly have to say to her, but she led him into the kitchen so that they could talk. Jo, Beth, and Amy followed.

"I'm sorry not to be able to sell you the Bible in the window," Mr. Marshall began. "Shortly after you left, it occurred to me that I had another book at a much lower cost that you might like. I have it with me, if you'd care to see it. Tomorrow being Sunday, and Christmas the next day, I thought it best if I brought it directly to you this evening. I hardly expected to be invited to supper."

"Oh, Mr. Marshall, I should dearly love to see it," Meg said. "It is so near to Christmas Day, and I fear I won't have any gift for Father." She looked at her younger sisters, who were clustered together, and suddenly got nervous.

"Why are you here?" she whispered to

them, knowing how little Mr. Marshall cared for girls under the age of ten.

"We were all going to pay for the book," Amy said. "Naturally, we wanted to know what Mr. Marshall had to say."

Meg looked anxiously at Mr. Marshall, but he only smiled.

"How much does the book cost?" Meg asked. "I have only the two dollars and seventy-five cents."

"Three dollars," Jo declared. "I did some odd jobs for Mr. Emerson today, and he paid me twenty-five cents."

"Three dollars is exactly the cost," Mr. Marshall said. He took the Bible out of his bag. It was nowhere near as splendid as the one in the shop window, but it was large and nicely printed, and had maps of all the locations mentioned in the Bible.

"Oh, yes," Meg said, examining it from cover to cover. "This would be just lovely. Thank you, Mr. Marshall. I'll go upstairs right now and give you the money."

"After supper will be fine," Mr. Marshall said.

They all went back into the parlor. Meg was

overjoyed, and Father and Marmee were smiling.

"I was just saying to my wife that my daughters have given me a truly wonderful gift," Father said.

"How do you know what it is?" Amy asked.

"Not that gift," Father said. "Although I know I'll like it also. No, I'm talking about the sacrifices they have made, parting with their money to purchase something for me. And almost as splendid, they have brought into the house a man I was looking forward to meeting, a man whose friendship I hope to cultivate. Perhaps, if you have no other plans for Christmas Day, you might honor us with your presence at our Christmas dinner."

"It is I who would be honored," Mr. Marshall replied. "In fact, now that I've met all your daughters, I may have to change my rules and let children under the age of ten into my shop."

"It's all right, Mr. Marshall," Jo said. "As long as you don't sell hair ribbons, you won't be bothered by the youngest of us."

As all of them, even Amy, laughed, Meg

looked at her family and their new friend. Father and Marmee might not have great riches as did Aunt March, but they truly were happy as kings. And Meg, knowing that she had added to their happiness, felt richest of all.

Jo's
Christmas
Dream

Last year Meg told me that Marmee used to write a letter to herself at Christmastime. So Meg wrote one. Now I've decided to do the same thing because I plan on being a famous author someday and others might be curious to know what Christmas was like for me as a girl. (I should dearly love to read Marmee's Christmas letters, even though she isn't a famous author.)

I have spent much of my time lately writing plays. Most recently I completed "The Bride of Castlemere," which I do believe is my absolute best effort so far. I thought about calling it "The Duke's Revenge," but then it turned out the duke never got revenge. I, of course, will play the duke when we perform the play Christmas night. Meg will play the bride, and Amy will play our long-lost daughter. Bethy, who doesn't like to act, will accompany us on the piano. The cast will outnumber the audience, since only Father, Marmee, and Hannah will be in attendance.

I wonder what I'll get for Christmas. We'll hang our stockings up Christmas Eve and see how they're filled the next morning. I should love some candy and writing supplies and books. I know that won't all fit in a stocking, and I know there isn't much money for presents, but Christmas is such a special time, I'm sure I'll love whatever I'm given.

Aunt March invited me to her house last week and showed me a cameo that belonged to my great-grandmother. She said that she was going to give it to one of us, but she hadn't yet decided whom, and that I shouldn't mention it to any of the others.

She let me hold it, and it was thrilling to touch something that Father's grandmother had worn. I've never owned any real jewelry, and I should love it if Aunt March gave me the cameo. The two of us do squabble, but sometimes I think she truly likes me, so perhaps she would entrust me with such a wonderful gift.

Oh, dear. My biographers (and I'm sure there will be many of them) will *think I'm just a greedy, selfish child. I'm not. Books and a cameo will do me fine this Christmas.*

Jo March

CHAPTER 1

"*M*armee! Marmee!"

"No, no, Amy," Jo said in disgust. "Not Marmee. Call her Mother."

"But I call our mother Marmee," Amy said. "Why can't I call this mother Marmee as well?"

"Because she's a duchess," Jo said. "You were separated from her at birth by the evil count. So she's a stranger and not someone you're likely to call Marmee. Do you know what I mean?"

"I'm sure I don't," Amy said. "If I don't know to call her Marmee, perhaps I should call her Duchess."

Meg giggled. "It's funny enough to hear you

call me Mother," she said to her youngest sister. "I don't know what I'd do if you called out 'Duchess! Duchess!' instead."

" 'Mother' will do just fine," said Jo. "Amy, please."

"Mother, Mother," Amy repeated. "Oh, Jo, when will I be old enough to play the duchess?"

"Not for years to come," Jo replied.

"Jo will have written lots of other plays by then," said Beth, who was seated at the piano.

"True enough," said Jo. "But *The Bride of Castlemere* might just be my best."

"I do love playing the duchess," Meg said. "What is my next line, Jo? After Amy says, 'Mother, Mother'?"

" 'Oh, my dearest child,' " Jo said.

"That's right," Meg said. "Oh, my dearest child. How it thrills me to hold you in my arms once again and hear you call me by that most sacred of names, Mother."

"Can this be?" Jo asked. "My beloved wife, Rosalinda, and my long-lost daughter in her arms once again?"

"Father!" cried Amy.

"My dearest love," said Meg. "Here we are, reunited at last."

"The beautiful bride of Castlemere," said Jo. "A bride no longer, but a beauty forever. . . . The end."

Beth played an appropriate trill on the piano. Meg, Amy, and Jo practiced their bows to the imaginary sound of applause.

"It really is a wonderful play," Beth said. "I love the part where you wrestle with Lord Commonstock, Jo."

"I don't," said Meg. "It's hard to change from the beautiful bride to the evil lord, and Jo wrestles hard."

"I'd wrestle myself if I could," Jo said. "It would be so much easier to write plays if just one of my sisters were a brother."

"I'm not about to become a boy, thank you," said Amy. "Especially now, at Christmastime. What gifts do boys get? Toy soldiers. Cricket bats. I want hair ribbons and pretty lace, and I should dearly love my very own mirror."

"For you to waste more time admiring yourself," Jo said. "You're vain enough with one mirror in this house, Amy. Your very own, and we should never see you again."

"I shouldn't like to be a boy either," said Beth. "They're so rough-and-tumble."

"And I've always dreamed of being a wife and mother," said Meg. "Which would be impossible if I were a boy."

"It's not that I want to be a boy, either," Jo said. "Not really. But boys get to do so much more than girls. They get to have adventures, work as cabin boys on whaling ships and see the world. I wouldn't mind the work if I could only have the adventure that goes with it."

"Aunt March sees the world," Amy said. "She's traveled to New York and London and Paris. And she's never had to work to do it."

"Aunt March has money," said Jo.

"But perhaps one day she'll take you on one of her trips," Beth said. "Then you could see the world without working, Jo."

"Accompanying Aunt March would be work enough," Jo replied. "But I'd do it gladly if it meant a chance to see faraway places."

"Aunt March would never pick you to go with her," said Amy. "She's always trying to improve your manners, Jo."

"Perhaps so I'll be ready to travel with her,"

said Jo. "The more I think about it, the likelier it seems. I'm brave and strong. I could carry Aunt March's bags and help if we got lost."

"It will never happen," Amy said.

"If Jo wants it enough, it might," said Meg. "But Jo, you have to convince Aunt March that you're a suitable companion for her. And that might not be so easy."

"It could take years," Jo said. "So I think I'll start right now!"

CHAPTER 2

"Josephine," said Aunt March that very afternoon. "Why have you chosen to visit me today? Are you hoping perhaps for some early Christmas goody? There is still one day before Christmas, you know."

"I know, Aunt March," Jo said as she settled into a chair. She had spent the entire walk from her house to Aunt March's coming up with a reason for the visit and had finally worked one out. "Although Christmas is partly why I'm here," she added.

"I'm not surprised," said Aunt March. "And what about Christmas is it that brings you round?"

"An invitation," Jo said. "You know, of course, you're invited to Christmas dinner at our house."

"I know," said Aunt March.

"I hope you'll be attending," Jo said. "After dinner my sisters and I will be enacting my latest play, *The Bride of Castlemere*. It's absolutely the best thing I've ever written. It's set in Castlemere, which I believe is in Scotland."

"I can't say I've ever heard of the place," said Aunt March.

"I haven't either," Jo said. "Not really. But it sounded as if it should be in Scotland, and that's why I set it there. Of course, since you've traveled all over, you could tell me if what I've imagined comes close to the truth. I know I'd be a much better writer if I got to see the world, but since I'm too young to travel, a woman of your experience could be a great help to me."

"I'm sure I could be," said Aunt March. "But I intend to leave your home immediately following dinner. I don't care to be out at night this time of year. It gets dark awfully early, and there is always the risk of a winter storm."

"Couldn't you make an exception this one time?" asked Jo. "You could stay in my room.

Meg and I could sleep with Beth and Amy, so you'd have complete privacy."

"I think not," said Aunt March. "Now tell me the real reason for this visit, Josephine."

"What do you mean?" Jo asked.

Aunt March shook her head. "In all of your ten years, you have never been able to deceive me, and there is no point in trying to do so now."

"I've never tried to deceive you," Jo said. "And I have no idea what you're talking about." But then she realized she had in a way been trying to deceive Aunt March, and she blushed.

"Aha," said Aunt March. "Your face betrays you. You're here to see if I intend to give you the cameo brooch."

"What cameo?" asked Jo. "Oh, Great-grandmother's. I had forgotten all about it."

"You had what?" asked Aunt March.

Jo shrugged. "I've been so busy with the play," she said. "And school. And making Christmas presents for Father and Marmee. For you too, Aunt March. I've hardly thought of the cameo at all." She hoped that was the answer Aunt March was looking for.

But it didn't seem to be. "I want you to know, Josephine, that I seriously considered giving you that cameo," Aunt March declared. "But it's exactly this sort of thoughtlessness that convinces me it would be a mistake."

"I don't understand," Jo said.

"And you never will," Aunt March said. "Why can't you be more like your sisters? Even little Amy has more sense of what is proper than you do. Go home, Josephine. Once again, you have proven a terrible disappointment to me."

"And you to me," said Jo, rising from her chair. "For all I wanted was your presence at my Christmas play. I should think you'd be grateful for the invitation. But instead you insult me and throw me out."

"Don't you use that tone of voice with me, young lady!" Aunt March said.

"Then don't force me to," said Jo. "Very well. You want me out. I'm leaving." She stormed out of Aunt March's parlor, stopped only to get her coat and mittens, and ran out of the house. The farther away she got from Aunt March, the angrier she became. She hardly even felt the flakes of snow that landed gently on her face as she

60

ran home. How could she ever have expected Aunt March to do anything for her? The woman wouldn't even give her a cameo brooch. It would go to Amy, Jo was sure of it. Amy got everything she wanted, and all that Jo wanted as well. Amy was Aunt March's little pet, and Amy would no doubt get to see Europe by Aunt March's side while Jo stayed home, mending and cleaning and cooking.

"Jo, where were you?" asked Meg as Jo entered the house.

"Why do you need to know?" Jo asked angrily. She removed her coat and shook off the snow. "Are you keeping track of my every movement?"

"No, of course not," Meg said. "It's only that Amy—"

"Amy what?" Jo asked, not even giving Meg a chance to finish her sentence. "Amy's always wanting something. What is it this time? A diamond necklace?"

"No, of course not," Meg said.

"Whatever it is, I don't care!" Jo cried. "You can tell Her Majesty Amy that."

"Whatever's gotten into you, Jo?" Meg asked.

"Nothing." Jo sighed. "Except an awareness of how unfair everything is. You always get what you want, Meg, because you're the oldest. And Amy gets what she wants because she's the youngest. And Beth doesn't want anything, so she's never unhappy. But when I want something, well, what do I get? Nothing, that's what! I'm tired of doing for others and getting nothing in return. It's unfair!"

"But Jo," Meg said, "that simply isn't true."

"Are you calling me a liar?" Jo asked. "Oh, that's too much, even for me, to be called deceptive twice in one day. I hate this life. I hate everything about it. Now get out of my path, Meg. I don't want to speak to you ever again."

"Be that way," said Meg as Jo stamped up the stairs. "Ruin Christmas for all of us with your terrible temper. I can see that's what you want."

Jo spun around. "And why not?" she replied bitterly. "My Christmas is ruined already. Why should yours be any better?" She flew up the remaining stairs, past her bedroom, and into the attic, where only the heat of her rage kept her warm.

CHAPTER 3

"Josephine. Josephine March."

Jo looked up from her writing desk. Only Aunt March used that tone with her. And Aunt March never came up into the attic. What could be going on?

"I'm speaking to you, Josephine."

Jo turned around. It was definitely Aunt March, but she was dressed in a way Jo had never seen before. "Aunt March," Jo whispered. "Are you all right? You look like a ghost."

"I am a ghost," Aunt March replied. "I am the Ghost of Christmas Past."

Jo sat upright. "That's from *A Christmas Carol*," she said. "Father read it to us last year.

We all loved it, but I must admit I prefer Mr. Dickens's *Pickwick Papers*."

"I don't believe I asked for your opinion," said the Ghost of Christmas Past.

"No, Aunt March," Jo said. "I mean, Ghost of Christmas Past."

"Let us travel now to Christmas of a year ago," said the ghost, "and see how you behaved last year."

"I had a good time last year," Jo said. "I'd enjoy seeing it again."

"Very well," said the ghost. She clapped her hands twice, and before Jo knew it she was gazing down into the parlor of her home, watching her sisters and parents and herself standing around the piano, singing joyous Christmas songs.

"Beth, you play the piano better every Christmas," Jo heard herself say.

"I love to play for all of you," Beth said.

"And we love to hear you play," said Marmee. "And speaking of plays, Jo, your latest effort was your best. I shiver whenever I think of *The Ghost of Merrymore*."

"I'm sorry I forgot my lines," said Amy. "I'll try harder next time, Jo."

"That made me so angry," Jo said to the Ghost of Christmas Past. "Amy had plenty of time to learn her lines. And she only had three of them. But she could never get them right. She just about ruined my play."

"See how you dealt with your anger last year," replied the ghost.

Jo looked back down. She saw herself glaring at Amy and waited to hear her angry words.

"That's all right," she heard herself say instead. "It was your first big part, Amy. I'm sure you'll get better with more practice."

"Thank you, Jo," Amy said. "I don't think I'll ever be as good an actress as you or Meg, but I do want to try."

"I think all my little women are fine performers," said Father. "And it was very clever of you, Jo, to cover for Amy when she forgot her lines. I must say I was hardly aware of any problem at all."

"I did do a good job with that, didn't I?" said Jo. "But Meg helped also, and so did you, Bethy, playing the piano loudly just then."

"The theater is like a family," said Father. "When one member has a problem, the others step in and help."

"I sometimes think our family is like theater," said Marmee. "Full of comedy and drama."

"Someday when I'm a great writer, my plays will be performed in New York," Jo said. "Will you be proud of me then, Father?"

"I'm proud of you right now, Jo," Father replied. "You not only wrote the play, you performed in it, and you didn't let any setbacks disturb you. I'm as proud of you this very moment as I have ever been."

"I didn't even remember Father saying that," Jo said to the Ghost of Christmas Past. "How could I have forgotten such a wonderful thing? I remembered being angry at Amy for forgetting her lines, but not Father saying how proud of me he was."

"That's precisely why I'm here," said the Ghost of Christmas Past. "Memory is selective. It's good to force oneself to ask certain questions."

Jo shook her head. "Father's words were the best present I got," she said. "But all I could remember was my anger."

"Think about that, Josephine," the Ghost of Christmas Past demanded. And then, like a puff of smoke, she was gone.

CHAPTER 4

"Jo! Jo, come in here right now!"

Jo turned around. She was no longer in the attic. Somehow she had been transported into the kitchen, and it was Hannah's sharp voice that she heard.

"Yes, Hannah?" Jo asked. "Do you need me to help?"

"I'm not Hannah," Hannah said. "I'm the Ghost of Christmas Present."

Jo looked at Hannah. She too wore a ghostly shroud. In one hand she held a paring knife, in the other a potato.

"I'm still willing to help," said Jo. "Do you want me to peel that potato?"

"There's no need," said the Ghost of Christmas Present. And sure enough, Jo watched as the potato appeared to peel itself.

"Oh, my," said Jo. "How did you do that?"

"There are some advantages to being a ghost," said the ghost. "But I'm not here to perform parlor tricks for you."

"That looked more like a kitchen trick to me," Jo said. She felt more comfortable with the Ghost of Christmas Present. While it was true that Hannah had on more than one occasion scolded her roundly for her bad behavior, she had never made Jo feel as miserable as Aunt March had.

"This is not an occasion for humor," said the ghost. "I am here to show you the consequences of your behavior."

"Very well," said Jo. "But I'm sure the consequences can't be too bad."

"Don't be so sure," said the ghost. "Gaze upon your family as they are this very moment."

Without warning, the wall between the kitchen and the parlor disappeared. Jo could see right into the room. Her whole family was there, but Jo herself was nowhere to be seen.

"I don't understand, Marmee," Meg said.

"Jo was so angry when she got home. I never even had the chance to tell her what Amy wanted."

"She probably wanted something that rightfully should be mine," Jo said to the ghost. "Amy always wants what I have. Amy wants what everyone has." She looked back toward the parlor and saw Amy looking quite upset.

"Was it my fault?" Amy asked. "Maybe I should have spoken to Jo first."

"When Jo gets into one of her tempers, it's best if I speak to her," said Beth. "Perhaps if I'd been the one to greet her, she would have taken her anger out on me. When she does that, she feels so bad afterward, she's nice for days and days."

"Does Beth really feel that way?" Jo asked the ghost.

"I'm not here to answer your questions," the ghost replied. "I'm simply here to show you how your family is feeling because of you at this very moment."

"Girls, none of you is at fault," said Marmee. "If anyone is to blame, it's me."

"Marmee?" Jo said to the ghost. "But Marmee never does anything to hurt us."

71

"You might learn something if you listened," said the ghost.

"How could it be your fault, Marmee?" Meg asked. "You weren't even here when Jo came home."

"Perhaps I should have been," said Marmee. "I was bringing Christmas food to the poor, but if I'd been home, I could have asked Jo what the matter was, and perhaps I could have solved the problem before it spoiled Christmas for all of us."

"My dear, you're not at fault," said Father. "The fault, I fear, lies with me. I've always felt Jo's anger was the price she paid for her courage and strength. But her anger hurts her as much as it hurts the rest of us. I should have spoken to her about it long ago. I should have made her aware of the damage it can produce. It's my failing as a father that's the cause of all our pain."

"Oh, no, Father," Amy said. "I'm the one who made Jo angry. I never do anything right. I should have asked Jo myself if we could have one more rehearsal before tomorrow night's performance. But I was so busy reading the play and doing my best to memorize my lines that I made Meg ask for me. Jo misunderstood. I'll go up to the attic right now and try to make amends. I'd hate for Jo's anger at me to ruin Christmas for all of us."

"Don't go now," said Marmee. "Jo's a good girl, and I'm sure she'll come to her senses soon enough. Let's leave her alone and try to enjoy Christmas Eve without her. Beth, dearest, why don't you play the piano for us?"

"All right, Marmee," Beth said. "But our singing is never as nice without Jo."

"Nothing is," said Meg. "I do wish she'd come downstairs."

"She will in time," said Marmee. "Now, let's all sing and think of the joy of this occasion."

Jo's eyes watered and a few tears trickled down her face. "They're all so unhappy," she whispered to the ghost. "And it's all because of me, isn't it?"

"I believe you've answered your own question," said the ghost. And before Jo had a chance to say anything more, the ghost vanished, leaving Jo in the cold and empty kitchen.

CHAPTER 5

"Jo? Can you hear me, Jo?"

Jo whirled around. Only Beth used that loving tone with her. "Bethy? Where are you?"

"Over here, Jo," Beth replied.

It was dark in the kitchen, and it took a moment for Jo to make Beth out. She was standing in the corner, wearing the same ghostly shroud Jo had seen on Aunt March and Hannah.

"You too, Beth?" Jo asked.

Beth nodded. "I'm the Ghost of Christmas Yet to Come."

"I don't like the idea of your being a ghost," said Jo. "Why does it have to be you?"

"I don't know," the ghost said. "I was just

told to be here. And since it's to help you, I was happy to agree. Come with me, Jo, and see what your future Christmas will be like."

"I've seen last year and this year," Jo said. "I suppose this will be Christmas next year." She reached out to take Beth's hand but found it was as unsubstantial as fog.

"No, we're going to go far into the future," said the ghost. "You'll learn more that way."

"This is really very exciting," Jo said. "It made me sad to see last year's Christmas, because I'd forgotten all the good things, and this year's was full of misery. But to see into the future is just the sort of adventure I never thought I'd have."

"Not all adventures end well," said the ghost. "Here we are, Jo. Look hard and you'll see what your future will be like."

Jo gazed down into the March family parlor on Christmas Day. Stockings hung on the mantel, and a small Christmas tree with lovely, colorful decorations had been placed on the table. Two children were sitting on the floor, admiring their presents. There were adults as well, and it took Jo a moment to recognize them.

"There's Marmee!" she cried in delight. "But look how gray her hair is. And Father. He looks so dignified. And who are those children? Is that grown woman with the blond curls Amy?"

"Yes, that's Amy," said the ghost. "Her daughter is sitting on Father's lap."

"Amy's a mother?" said Jo. "She's such a child."

"But this is the future," the ghost said. "Amy will be a happy and beautiful woman then."

"Is that her husband by her side?" Jo asked. "He certainly is a handsome man. He seems to love her very much."

"He loves her dearly, and she him," said the ghost.

"But Amy's so spoiled," said Jo.

"Amy has learned many lessons from her life," said the ghost. "She's worked hard to overcome her faults."

"And is that Meg?" asked Jo. "Oh, it must be. And those precious children, are they hers?"

"Her twins," said the ghost. "And the man talking with Marmee is her husband."

76

Jo smiled. "They all seem so happy and contented," she said, wishing she could be there with them. "But where are you, Bethy?"

"I'm not there that Christmas," said the ghost. "But I'm sure they're thinking of me."

"And where am I?" Jo asked. "I saw myself in Christmas Past. Can't I see myself in the future as well?"

"You'll see yourself soon enough," the ghost said.

Into the family scene walked a tall, well-dressed woman. As soon as she arrived, the mood in the room changed. Where before there had been happy chatter, now there was silence.

"I'm here," the woman announced. "I can't say you seem happy to see me. Come here, children, and greet your aunt March."

"That can't be Aunt March," Jo said. "She's too young."

"Hello, Aunt March," the children said. Jo could see how reluctant they were to greet the woman and kiss her cold, unloving face.

"Hello, Jo," said Meg. "Was your trip pleasant?"

"That's *me*?" Jo cried to the ghost. "*I'm* Aunt March?"

"That's what they call you," the ghost said. "Listen, Jo, and see how you've become. That's what you wanted, isn't it, to see yourself in the future?"

Jo nodded, but she didn't think she'd like anything she saw.

"My trip was tolerable," the grown-up Jo declared. "Still, it was a shame to leave New York. My latest play is a triumph, you know. Hello, Marmee, Father. I did mean to bring presents for all of you, but I've been so busy, I never had a chance to buy a single thing."

"We understand, Jo," said Marmee. "You know you don't have to bring us anything."

"I'll be off to Europe next week," said the grown-up Jo. "If I remember, I'll purchase some trinkets there for the children."

"I'm sure they'll appreciate that, Jo," said Meg. "Please sit down. Would you like something warm to drink?"

"I won't be staying very long," said the grown-up Jo. "I know you'll all be happier when I'm gone."

"Jo, I wish you didn't feel that way," said Marmee.

"I'm only speaking the truth," said the grown-up Jo. "I don't know why I even bothered to return today, except that it's Christmas and there was nowhere else to go. All my friends are celebrating with their families. I have many friends, you know. Of course because they're all successful, they're very busy, and I don't see much of them. But as long as my plays continue to bring in the crowds, I'll be able to call many people my friends."

"We're very proud of your success," said Father. "We hope someday to go to New York and see one of your plays."

"That's what you say every year," said the grown-up Jo. "But you're never willing to spend money on the trip. I suppose if I paid, you might come. Still, I don't truly believe that you've ever cared enough about me to revel in my success, have you, Father? None of you has. You stay in Concord and play with your grandchildren and don't bother to think about me at all. I mean nothing to you. Well, you're nothing to me either. I've never needed any of you, and I never will."

"Jo, please," said Marmee. "You're so wrong—"

"Don't try to defend yourselves," interrupted the grown-up Jo. "I'm leaving. I'll think of you when my next play opens and none of you bothers to attend. Good-bye."

In horror, Jo watched as her grown-up self swept out of the house. "Amy never even spoke to her," she said, refusing to acknowledge that horrible woman as herself.

"You and Amy had a dreadful quarrel," the ghost said. "You haven't exchanged a word since."

"How terrible!" Jo said. "When did I become so mean?"

"You've always been angry," said the ghost. "But as you got older, you got angrier. At this Christmas, even at home, you're alone and unloved."

"And that's my future?" Jo asked. "Must it be? Can't I do anything to change it?"

"What do you think you'd have to do?" the ghost asked.

"I should stop being so angry," Jo said. "And when I am angry at someone, I shouldn't take it out on another."

"Is that all?" the ghost asked.

Jo thought hard. "Today I was angry at Aunt March and I took it out on Meg," she said. "But the truth is I was angriest at myself. Aunt March can always see through me. I went there pretending I wanted her to see my play, but the truth was I wanted her to think of me as someone worthy of taking to Europe someday. I was being selfish, and though she didn't guess why, she did guess that I wasn't sincere. I didn't like myself, and I got angry at her and then at Meg. Oh, Bethy, I've been just terrible. No wonder no one loves me."

"I love you," the ghost said. "We all love you, Jo. Even Aunt March loves you in her own way. Why can't you realize that?"

"Because when I get angry, I feel as though no one could possibly love me," said Jo. "Then I get even angrier. If I keep it up, no one will love me, and I'll be even lonelier than Aunt March."

"I don't want that to happen," said the ghost. "None of us does, Jo. We want you to be the loving, happy girl you often are. Promise me you'll try, Jo."

"I promise," Jo said. "I promise I'll be better."

The ghost smiled. "The better you are, the better your future will be," she said. "I love you, Jo. No matter what happens, I'll always be with you, and I'll always love you."

Before Jo had the chance to tell Beth the same, the ghost of Christmas Yet to Come had vanished.

CHAPTER 6

Jo woke up with a start. She was sitting in the attic, her head resting against her writing desk. She realized she was shivering and felt sure it wasn't just because the attic was cold.

"Beth?" she called, as though she could recapture the ghostly presence of her sister. But she was all alone.

She could hear voices singing downstairs. "That's right," Jo said. "They're singing carols. But they're thinking of me. They all feel to blame for my awful behavior."

It took Jo a moment to remember how it was she knew what her family was feeling. But as images of her dream flashed before her, she could also picture that last horrible vision of Christmas Yet to Come.

"I will change," she vowed. "I won't let my anger get the better of me. I swear I'll work every day to be less angry and to be more loving. Even with Aunt March."

The first thing she had to do was go downstairs. Still, she didn't move. The attic was cold and dark, but the idea of apologizing to everybody was frightening.

"Oh, Bethy," Jo whispered. "It's easier to say I'm sorry if I don't mean to change. But it's not enough to apologize anymore. I have to be better so that there'll be less need for me to apologize."

But Beth wasn't there to respond.

Jo sighed. The hardest things to do were the things she had to do alone. But if she were to remain part of her loving family, she'd have to become worthy of them. No one could do that for her.

Slowly she walked out of the attic and down the stairs. As she approached the parlor, she could hear the singing get softer, as though her family were preparing for her arrival.

"Oh, Meg," Jo said as she entered the parlor. "Can you ever forgive me?"

"Of course," Meg said. "I just wish I knew what I had done."

"You did nothing," Jo said. "You're a loving sister. And Amy, I'm so proud of the way you keep improving as an actress, only I've never told you. Please forgive me for not seeming to notice."

"You're apologizing to me?" Amy asked.

Jo nodded. "Most humbly," she said.

"Then I forgive you," Amy said, and Jo didn't even mind her grand manner.

"And Beth," Jo said, "when I'm angry at others, you don't have to try to soothe me. I love it that you do, but I'm never angry at you. I love you so much."

"And I love you," said Beth.

"Marmee, Father," Jo said. "You're the best parents a girl could dream of. Marmee, I'm such a better person from watching all the good things you do for others, and I try to do them myself. And Father, you've always listened to my dreams and encouraged me and told me how proud you are of me. Those words mean so much. I hope you know how much I want you to be proud of me."

"I know, my child," said Father.

"Your love means the world to me," Jo said. "The love of my parents and my sisters. And I promise all of you, from now on I'll work harder to deserve that love. I'll try to keep my anger to myself and never take my bad moods out on you. That's my Christmas wish for this year and for all the Christmases to come."

"We're none of us perfect, Jo," said Marmee. "The important thing is to keep trying."

"I will," Jo said. "Tomorrow morning I'll go to Aunt March's and apologize to her. And then we'll all have Christmas dinner together, and we'll be the loving family I cherish so much."

"Dinner's ready," said Hannah, coming into the parlor. She didn't look anything like a ghost, Jo was pleased to see.

"Come, everyone," said Father, leading the way to the dinner table. "Tonight we have even more than we usually do to thank God for."

Jo smiled as she joined her family. Her heart was so full of song, she wasn't sure she could wait until after supper to go caroling. She had seen her past and present, and she knew her future would be much richer as a result.

Beth's Christmas Dream

Jo told me that Marmee used to write a letter to herself each Christmas and that she and Meg had taken to doing that as well. Jo thought perhaps I should write one, although I don't know who could possibly be interested in what I have to say.

"_You_ will be, when you're grown up," Jo told me. "Write it for yourself."

So I'm giving it a try, but it feels odd to be writing something I'll read when I'm a grown woman with children of my own. I wonder if Marmee reads her childhood Christmas letters. I don't see how she could find the time. She's so busy taking care of all of us and Father and helping the poor.

Still, Jo's ideas are almost always good. Of course, writing comes easily to her (her latest play, "Death Triumphs over Wickedness," is truly her best). And Meg is so sure she'll be happily married and a loving mother when she's older that it makes sense for her to write something she'll want to read years later.

But nothing I do now is important, and as for the future, I can never see it clearly. I'd like to picture myself married with children, but I can never envision what they might look like. Sometimes I look at my dolls and think of them as all the babies I will have, but most of them are missing arms or legs or even heads, and I certainly wouldn't want my children to be in such pitiful states!

So I don't know to whom I'm writing this, or why, but I will say we are all healthy and happy this Christmas. Meg grows more womanly each year, and Jo works harder and harder at controlling her temper, and Amy draws all the time in her determination to be a great artist. Marmee and Father are devoted to each other, to their daughters, and to their good works. Dear Hannah continues to care for us with love and kindness. And Aunt March watches over us, trying to make us worthy of the March family heritage.

There. I've written something. I wonder what I'll

think when I read this letter years from now. Meg will be a mother, and Jo a writer, and Amy an artist. Will I still be shy little Bethy who plays with her dolls? I wonder.

Beth March

CHAPTER 1

"Beth. Oh, Beth, dearest."

"Yes, Marmee?" Beth called from her bedroom. She was planning a special Christmas dinner for her little family of dolls and wanted them all to look their best when they sat down for the imaginary feast.

"Come down, dear," said Marmee.

Beth put the dolls back on their shelf and went downstairs. Marmee was in the parlor, standing by the fireplace. She was reading a note.

"This is from Aunt March," Marmee said. "She'd like you to pay a call on her."

"Me?" said Beth. Aunt March terrified her, and the thought of visiting filled her with dread.

"That's what the note says," Marmee replied. "She requests the pleasure of your company for tea this afternoon."

"But why would Aunt March want to see me?" Beth asked.

Marmee shook her head. "She doesn't say. She simply invites you to come. You don't have anything else planned, do you, Bethy?"

"No," Beth said. Meg and Jo and Amy all had friends they called on to play with, but Beth stayed home when she wasn't at school, and there was no reason she couldn't call on her great-aunt.

"Very well," said Marmee. "The weather is certainly pleasant enough. It's hardly snowed at all this December. Perhaps Aunt March has a special holiday treat in store for you." But she looked as doubtful as Beth felt.

Beth went back upstairs. Meg and Jo were in their bedroom. "May I come in?" Beth asked.

"You're always welcome," said Jo, who was sprawled on her bed reading a book. Meg was sitting on hers, doing some mending.

"What's the matter, Beth?" Meg asked. "You look flustered."

"Aunt March has invited me to tea," said Beth. "Just me."

"Poor child," said Jo.

"Shush," said Meg. "Aunt March isn't as bad as all that."

"Oh, yes, she is," said Jo with such fervor that they all laughed.

"I can't imagine why she'd want to see me," Beth said. "Aunt March never seems to know I exist."

"I'll wager I know what the reason is," said Jo.

"What?" asked Meg.

"The cameo brooch," Jo said.

"Oh, of course," said Meg, and then she and Jo laughed.

"What brooch?" Beth asked. "And what does it have to do with me?"

"Aunt March has in her possession a cameo brooch that belonged to Father's grand-mother," Meg replied. "She intends to give it to one of us, but she can't decide which one of us should be so honored."

"She's already decided against Meg and me," Jo said. "Now that you're ten, it must be your turn to be shown the brooch."

"But why wouldn't she give it to one of you?" Beth asked.

"After she showed it to me, I wanted it very badly in order to sell it and buy Father a certain Bible," Meg replied. "Aunt March didn't care for that at all."

"And I acted as though I didn't want it," said Jo. "She cared for that even less."

"You don't think she'd give it to me, do you?" asked Beth.

"I don't see why not," said Jo. "You certainly deserve it. You're the best of us all, Bethy, the sweetest, with the kindest heart. Why shouldn't you be given the cameo?"

"I may be sweet and have a kind heart," said Beth, "but I don't think those are virtues Aunt March particularly cares for."

The girls laughed again. "It will be easy for you to convince Aunt March to give you the cameo," said Meg. "All you have to do is act as though you don't want it and act as though you do."

"That sounds impossible," said Beth.

"Don't listen to her," Jo said. "Just be yourself, Bethy, and that will do very nicely. If Aunt March has decided she wants you to have the cameo, she'll give it to you no matter how you behave. If she's decided against you, nothing you can say will change her mind. Aunt March can't be outwitted, and there's no point trying."

"I would never try to do that," said Beth. How could she outwit Aunt March when it terrified her to be in the same room with her?

CHAPTER 2

"Come in, Beth," said Aunt March from her chair in the parlor. "Don't hang back there. The fire won't scorch you, and I want a better look at you."

"Yes, Aunt March," Beth said, wishing with all her heart that Father or Marmee or any one of her sisters was by her side. Slowly she made her way into the room until she stood before her imposing aunt.

"You haven't grown much," said Aunt March.

"No, Aunt March," Beth said. She knew it would be unwise to point out that Aunt March had seen her only last Sunday in church, and no one grew much in less than a week.

"Speak up," said Aunt March. "Whenever

you speak to me, Beth, I worry about my hearing."

"I'm sorry, Aunt March," Beth whispered. "I mean, I'm sorry," she nearly shouted.

"A normal conversational tone will do," said Aunt March. "Tell me, Beth, what do you do with yourself? How do you occupy your time?"

"I suppose I go to school and help out at home," Beth said.

"You suppose," said Aunt March. "Don't you know?"

Beth moved a step back. "Yes, Aunt March," she said. "I mean—That is to say, that's what I do."

"You're not one for parties, are you, girl?" said Aunt March. "Nor running around like a wild animal?"

"No, Aunt March," said Beth.

"Very well," said Aunt March. "I invited you here today to show you something." She picked up a small box from the table by her side and handed it to Beth. "This belonged to your great-grandmother March," she said. "My husband, your late uncle March, told me that it had been given to her, his mother, when she was a girl of ten. Which I believe is your age now."

"Yes, Aunt March," Beth said. She opened the box and looked at the cameo. It was quite the most beautiful piece of jewelry she had ever seen. "This truly belonged to Great-grandmother?" she asked.

Aunt March nodded.

"Did you know her?" Beth asked.

"She had died before I met Mr. March," Aunt March replied. "His father gave him the cameo to give to his bride. Of course, that was many years ago. I've held on to it, trying to determine which of my grandnieces should be its next owner. What do you think, Beth? Would you like it?"

"Very much," said Beth. "It's so beautiful. And I love the idea that it's been in our family for so many years. I'm sorry you never had the opportunity to meet Great-grandmother, Aunt March. I would have liked to learn more about what she was like."

"I like your answers, Beth. Rather more than I thought I would," said Aunt March.

"But I don't care to rush to a decision. So tell me, Beth, what would you do with the cameo if I gave it to you?"

"I don't know." Beth closed the box and handed it back to Aunt March. "I suppose I'd put it away for safekeeping and let my sisters wear it on special occasions."

"But you wouldn't wear it yourself?" Aunt March asked.

"I don't think so," Beth replied. "It's too fine to wear every day. And as you pointed out, I don't go to parties. No one would ever see it if I owned it, so my sisters might as well wear it whenever they wanted."

"Then there's no point in giving it to you," said Aunt March. "You'd make no use of it whatsoever."

"I wouldn't, I suppose," whispered Beth.

Aunt March shook her head. "I don't know what to make of you, child," she said. "Sometimes even when you're in the same room with me, you're so quiet, I forget you're there."

"I'm sorry, Aunt March," said Beth.

"Very well," Aunt March said. "Stay and have some tea, and then you can go home."

"Thank you," Beth said. It saddened her to

see Aunt March put the cameo away and to know it would never be hers. But she knew she didn't deserve such a beautiful piece of jewelry, and she was sure whoever did own it would be far worthier of the honor than she.

CHAPTER 3

"You didn't, Beth," said Jo that evening in her bedroom. "Aunt March practically gave you the cameo and you told her not to?"

"No," Beth said. "I told her I'd never wear it. And I wouldn't, Jo. Besides, it should have gone to you or Meg, or to Amy, if Aunt March offers it to her. You're all much more deserving than I am."

"I don't see why," Jo said.

"Meg is the oldest," Beth said. "She's nearly an adult, and she loves pretty things. She would wear the cameo and it would look perfect on her. And you're the bravest of us, the one who'll go out in the world someday and meet the most interesting people, and if you had the cameo, people would ask you about it and learn of Great-grandmother that way. And Amy is Aunt March's favorite. We all know that. Aunt March always smiles when Amy enters the room. So Aunt March should give her the cameo because she cares most for Amy. But I'm nothing, Jo. I stay at home and help Hannah, and that contents me. I'd stop going to school if Father would let me. If the cameo were mine it would sit in its box and never see the light of day. Aunt March didn't want that for it, and neither do I. No, it's best that Aunt March didn't give it to me."

"But didn't you want it?" Jo asked.

Beth nodded.

"Then you should have told Aunt March," Jo said. "Perhaps it would have made a difference. If you want, I'll go to Aunt March and ask her to give it to you."

"Oh, no," said Beth. "Please don't, Jo. It doesn't matter. I'm happy enough just to have seen the cameo, to have held it in my hand and thought of Great-grandmother getting it when she was ten. That was so special for me, Jo. Don't spoil it by getting into a quarrel with Aunt March."

"Very well," said Jo. "Although I suppose I'll get into a quarrel over something else with Aunt March soon enough, no matter how hard I try not to. But I admit I'm disappointed, Beth. I would have liked to see you wear that cameo at least once."

"Maybe I will someday," Beth said. "But I shouldn't be its owner."

"Which means Amy will be, I suppose," Jo said. "Oh, well. She doesn't suffer from false modesty. If Aunt March gives the brooch to her, she'll assume it's her rightful possession and treat it accordingly."

Beth nodded. There were times she wished she could be more like Amy, just as there were times she wished she were more like Meg or Jo. Braver, more outgoing, funnier, better liked. She tried to picture herself that way, all dressed for a party, wearing the cameo as though it naturally belonged to her, but she couldn't make the image last. She was quiet, mousy Beth, whom no one much cared about.

"Did I hear my name?" Amy asked, walking into Jo's room. "What are you two talking about?"

"It's a secret," said Jo. "And besides, you're not old enough to know."

"I hate it when you say that," Amy said. "If Beth's old enough, then I am too. Don't tease me, Jo."

"We have a secret and Amy's too young," Jo chanted.

"Stop that, Jo," Beth said. "I'm afraid it is a secret, Amy, and not ours to tell. You know I would if I could, but if I broke a confidence, you would never trust me with your secrets."

"I suppose," Amy said. "But I don't see why Jo has to be so mean about it."

"Tell her you're sorry, Jo," said Beth. "Amy's right, you know. You were being mean."

"All right," Jo said. "I'm sorry, Amy. But you shouldn't have been eavesdropping."

"I wasn't eavesdropping," Amy said. "I was merely listening without being invited." She looked quite righteous for a moment, and then she laughed along with her sisters.

"I'll go see if Hannah needs any help with supper," Beth said. "Jo? Amy? Do you want to join me?"

"No, thank you," they both said.

Beth sighed. Jo and Amy had other, more important things to do. But she might as well be useful in the kitchen. It was the best she had to offer.

CHAPTER 4

*B*eth lay still in bed that night, thinking about her family. She could hear Amy's quiet breathing by her side. Amy never seemed to have trouble sleeping, but some nights Beth found sleep close to impossible. There was so much to worry about, especially when it was dark and everyone else in the house was asleep. Would there be a war? Would her sisters grow up and find men to marry? Would Father and Marmee stay healthy? Would Hannah find her work too burdensome? Would it snow, would it rain, would the garden flourish, would the kittens grow, would all be as it should be, or would horrible changes occur? Sometimes Beth wondered how anyone could sleep with so many unanswered and unanswerable questions around.

"Beth March."

Beth sat up. She couldn't imagine who would be calling her name in the middle of the night.

"Beth March, I want you to come with me."

"Quiet," Beth said as she squinted and caught sight of a vague bodily shape. "Don't wake up Amy."

"Amy will be fine," the voice said. "Get out of bed, Beth, and follow me."

Beth did as she was told. She put on her robe and slippers and followed the form out of her bedroom. Together they walked silently down the stairs and into the kitchen, which was still warm from the woodstove. The figure held up a candle, and Beth could make out an older man with a bushy white beard. He was dressed in furs and was smoking a small pipe.

"Do you know who I am?" he asked.

"St. Nicholas?" Beth asked.

The man nodded. "Ever since Clement Moore wrote that poem about me, I am more easily recognized," he said. "Merry Christmas, Beth."

"Merry Christmas to you, sir," said Beth. "Would you care for something to eat?"

"No, thank you," St. Nicholas said. "I'm here for a very special reason. It's been brought to my attention that you're in need of a service only I can perform."

Beth looked bewildered. "Thank you very much. But I'm sure I don't need any sort of service."

"That's not what I've been told." St. Nicholas smiled. "A certain mutual friend of ours told me about the cameo brooch Aunt March showed you. She said you didn't think you were worthy of such a fine gift."

"I'm not," Beth said. "Did Jo tell you that?"

"I'm not at liberty to disclose that," said St. Nicholas. "Tell me, Beth. Have you ever thought about what the world would be like if you had never been born?"

"No," Beth said. "But I don't think it would be very much different."

"I beg to differ," St. Nicholas replied. "Sometimes it's the quiet ones who make the biggest difference."

"I'm not sure I believe that," Beth said. "But even if it's true, I'm sure it doesn't apply to me. No one even knows I'm alive except for my family."

"But your family is your world," St. Nicholas said. "How do you think they'd feel if you'd never been born?"

Beth thought about it. She knew her parents and sisters loved her dearly. But still . . . "I'm sure they'd be just the same without me," she said. "Meg would be just as sweet, and Jo just as smart, and Amy just as charming. Marmee and Father would be every bit as happy. Perhaps even happier, since they'd have one less mouth to feed. It's true, I help Hannah out, but without me, there'd be one less person to cook for and clean up after, so I doubt she'd miss me, either. And Aunt March certainly wouldn't. Everything would be exactly the same if I hadn't been born. I'm afraid you were sent here for no reason, St. Nicholas. Perhaps you should go, and I'll go back to bed."

"My mission is not yet done," St. Nicholas declared. "My purpose here tonight is to show you just what your family would be like if you *had* never been born, Beth March. Are you ready for that journey?"

"All right," Beth said, but she was just being polite. She knew how little she mattered. Everything was certain to be the same even if she'd never been born.

CHAPTER 5

"I believe you know this place," St. Nicholas said to Beth as they stood in the Marches' parlor.

"Of course," Beth said. "It's home."

"Ho ho ho," he laughed. "Look more closely. Do you see any differences?"

"It's daytime," Beth said. "And it was nighttime just moments ago."

"I have certain powers," St. Nicholas told her. "There's more to me than giving presents to children, you know."

"No, I didn't know," said Beth. "Is that all the difference?"

"Look around," St. Nicholas said. "It's your home. You know it best."

Beth looked carefully. The parlor wasn't as tidy as it usually was. The photograph of Father, taken by Mathew Brady, wasn't in its customary place on the wall. And then Beth gasped. Her piano, the one she dearly loved and played so often, was gone.

"Where's my piano?" she asked.

"The Marches have no need for it," said St. Nicholas. "After all, you were the one who played."

"But we sang every night," said Beth. "How can we all sing without the piano?"

"This March family doesn't care to sing," he replied. "Tell me, Beth, who are these people?"

"Marmee and Meg, of course," Beth said, watching as her mother and sister entered the parlor. But she could see a difference in them immediately. Marmee, who always dressed so neatly, looked almost slovenly. And Meg, who never fought with anyone, was enraged.

"You can't stop me!" Meg shouted at Marmee. "I'll see whomever I want whenever I want."

"You're making a terrible mistake," Marmee

said. "Meg, listen to me. You think your friends are good because they have riches. But they're not good, and they'll hurt you."

"What do you know about friends?" Meg said. "Or good times? They like me and I like them. I hate being in this house. Do you hear me? I hate it, and I'm going where I'm wanted. Don't try to stop me!" She pushed Marmee aside and ran out of the house.

"Meg, wait!" Beth cried, but neither Meg nor Marmee seemed to hear her. "St. Nicholas," she said, "they don't know I'm here."

"You don't exist," St. Nicholas pointed out. "How can they possibly hear someone who doesn't exist?"

"But why were they fighting?" Beth asked. "Why is Meg so unhappy?"

"I think you'll find the answer to that question if you just wait," St. Nicholas replied. "Who are those people entering the room now?"

"That's Jo and Amy," Beth said. They certainly looked like Jo and Amy, but she had never seen them behave quite so dreadfully. Jo was pulling one of Amy's curls, and Amy

117

was crying in pain and trying to reach back and punch Jo.

"Girls, girls," Marmee said, but Beth could see she had no hope of stopping her daughters from their wretched behavior.

"Mother, make Jo stop!" Amy cried.

"Why does she call her Mother?" Beth asked. "We've always called her Marmee."

"Marmee is a name of love," St. Nicholas replied. "Do you see any love in this room?"

"Little pig," Jo said before Beth had a chance to reply. "Mother, Amy was eating my food again. She's always stealing from me. If I don't beat her, she'll never stop."

"Do what you must," Marmee said. "Only please stop being so noisy about it. I have a terrible headache."

"Ha!" Jo shouted. "Did you hear that, you little wretch? You'll get that beating you deserve now!"

"Don't be so sure of that!" Amy shouted back. She freed herself from Jo's grasp, grabbed a shoe from one of her feet, and flung it at Jo, who just barely avoided being hit.

"I'll really get you now," Jo said. She

chased Amy around the parlor, her arms swinging out every which way. But instead of grabbing Amy, Jo knocked two little china figurines from the mantel.

"Mother!" Amy screamed as she took cover behind a chair. "Jo's breaking the china again!"

"Oh, dear," said Marmee. "Hannah! Come in here right away and clean up this mess."

Hannah entered the parlor. She too looked just the same but not quite right. Beth quickly realized she'd never seen such an expression of sullen resentment on Hannah's face. "What is it now?" Hannah asked.

"Jo broke the china, Jo broke the china," Amy chanted.

"I'll break *you* when I have a chance," said Jo. "You little beast."

"Well?" said Marmee. "What are you waiting for, Hannah? Clean it up."

" 'Clean it up, clean it up,' " Hannah repeated. "As though there isn't mess enough around here. Jo's the one who broke it. Why don't you make her clean it up?"

"Mother can't make me do anything I don't want to," Jo said. "And I don't want to."

Marmee sighed. "Aunt March is due here any minute," she said. "Hannah, clean up the mess, and then go to the kitchen and see what you can do about preparing us some tea."

"You expect me to do the work of five around here," Hannah grumbled. She bent down and picked up some of the bigger pieces of china. "There," she said. "That'll have to do." With that, she walked out of the parlor.

"Jo, please clean up the mess you made," Marmee said. "Aunt March does hate it so when things aren't tidy."

"And I hate Aunt March," said Jo. "If it's so important that the house be tidy, then clean it up yourself. I have to catch Amy and beat her for stealing from me."

"It was just a crust of bread," said Amy. "Mother, why doesn't Father come home anymore and bring us money for food?"

Marmee rubbed her forehead. "I don't know, Amy," she said. "Oh, that must be Aunt March. Would you open the door, please?"

"I don't feel like it," Amy said.

Marmee sighed and walked out of the parlor to open the front door. "Aunt March," she said. "Please come in."

Aunt March, at least, looked exactly like Aunt March. "I see things are just as they were when I was here last," she said. "A mess as always."

"Auntie March, Auntie March," Amy said, running to her and hugging her. "Oh, Auntie March, I love you so. Please take me home to live with you."

"I just may do that, Amy, dearest," said Aunt March. "Look at you. When was the last time you ate?"

"Yesterday," Amy said. "Jo hoards all the food and never shares with anyone."

"This is all your fault," Aunt March said to Marmee. "No decent, self-respecting woman would let her children behave like wild animals. Where is Margaret?"

"Out," Marmee said.

"She's just a child, but already she has a reputation," said Aunt March. "Josephine, come here this minute."

"I will not," said Jo, hiding behind the china cupboard. "And you can't make me, you wicked old witch."

"Did you hear that?" Amy cried. "Oh,

Auntie March, Jo is so dreadful. You must take me home with you. You simply must."

"I am forced to agree," Aunt March declared. "Go upstairs and get your few pathetic belongings, Amy."

Amy raced up the stairs, avoiding Jo's outstretched hands only by the quickness of her movements.

"This household is a disgrace," Aunt March said to Marmee. "It's no wonder my nephew has left. Amy isn't much, but she's the best of your three daughters. Perhaps under my guidance and care, she will be saved from the destiny that awaits Margaret." She took a quick look at Jo and shuddered. "The gallows will be her fate, I'm sure," she said.

"Oh, well," said Marmee, not seeming to care at all that Aunt March was stealing her youngest away from her. "At least with Amy gone, there'll be one less mouth to feed."

"I'm not surprised to hear you say that," said Aunt March. "Come, Amy. Let me take you to a decent household and teach you what a true lady should know. I think it would be best if you never saw your mother or sisters again."

"Thank you, thank you, Auntie March," said Amy. She gave Jo a quick kick before running out of the house.

"Hurrah!" cried Jo as Amy and Aunt March departed. "I'll never have to see either of them again."

"I will miss Amy, I suppose," Marmee said with a sigh. "Still, things should be quieter around here without her. And Meg soon will run off, I'm sure."

"I will too," Jo said. "Or would you rather I stayed, Mother? I wouldn't mind that nearly as much, now that Amy's gone forever."

"I'm sure I don't care," said Marmee. "You'll do whatever you want, regardless of my wishes."

But Jo wasn't listening. Beth watched as she ran into the kitchen, grabbed an apple, and ran out of the house. Hannah followed her, waving a knife angrily.

"That apple was to be our supper!" Hannah shouted. "It will truly be a merry Christmas this year."

"Oh, please," Beth said to St. Nicholas. "Do I have to keep watching?"

"There's nothing more to see," he replied. "You may go back to bed now, Beth, and think about what you've just witnessed."

Beth walked back to her bedroom alone. She stood for a moment by her bed and saw Amy sleeping peacefully. Then she noticed herself in bed. Not knowing how she did it, Beth silently reentered her body and fell into a deep, dreamless sleep.

CHAPTER 6

"Beth. Bethy. Wake up, dearest."

Beth woke up with a start to find Marmee sitting on her bed. "I was beginning to think I'd never rouse you from your sleep," Marmee said.

"Oh, Marmee!" Beth cried as she reached out to embrace her mother.

"What brings this on?" Marmee asked, stroking Beth's hair. "Did you have a nightmare?"

"I did," Beth said. "At least I think I did. Marmee, where's Father?"

"In his study, going over his Christmas sermon one last time," Marmee replied.

"And Meg? Where's Meg?"

"She's in the parlor with Jo," said Marmee. "Wrapping presents. I'm not sure, but I think there are one or two for you!"

"And Amy," Beth said. "She was asleep here last night. I remember that much. But where is she now?"

"In the kitchen, trying to help Hannah bake the Christmas cookies," said Marmee.

"And they're all happy?" Beth asked.

"Of course they are," said Marmee. "Today is Christmas Eve. We have so much to celebrate, how can we not be happy?"

"Oh, Marmee," Beth said. She held her mother even more tightly. "I had the strangest dream last night. I dreamed I didn't exist."

"That *is* a nightmare," Marmee said. "How could I live without my sweet Beth?"

"It was awful," Beth said. "Everyone was so angry at each other. Marmee, am I that important?"

"Of course you are," said Marmee. "Didn't you know that, Beth?"

"No," Beth said. "I thought all I did was help with the housework sometimes."

Marmee kissed Beth's forehead. "You do far

more than that," she said. "You bring joy to your father by the sweetness of your nature. You make Meg feel important because of the way you look up to her. Your gentle love keeps Jo from misbehaving. And your very presence prevents Amy from being spoiled."

"Really?" Beth asked. "I do all that?"

"And more," Marmee said. "You help Hannah without having to be asked. And as for me, my darling Bethy, I couldn't imagine life without your smile to greet me every morning."

"I knew you all loved me," Beth said. "But I never thought about why."

"Sometimes when we love people, we take them for granted," said Marmee. "And we forget to tell them why they're special. I'm sorry, Bethy, if that's happened to you."

"It's all right, Marmee," Beth said. "Because now I know why I'm special. Thanks to you and St. Nicholas."

"St. Nicholas was here?" Marmee asked.

Beth nodded.

Marmee smiled. "I'm glad he knows how special you are also," she said. "Now, do you plan to spend all of Christmas Eve in bed or are you going to join your family in celebration?"

Beth leaped out from under the sheets. "It's Christmas Eve," she said. "And I have more to celebrate than I ever knew there could be."

Amy's
Christmas
Dream

Meg, Jo, and Beth each came to me last week and said that Marmee used to write a letter to herself at Christmastime, and that they have been doing the same thing. They encouraged me to join in the tradition. I don't know why they always think what's good for them is good for me, but I don't see any harm in writing a few words down. Perhaps it will also please Marmee. Here goes . . .

Last year around Christmas I caught Jo and Beth exchanging a confidence that had something to do with me. I spent much of the year pretending I didn't remember and was able to pick up bits and pieces of information by seeming ignorant. (I have learned a great deal over the years that way.) It seems Aunt March has a piece of jewelry that belonged to Father's grandmother, and she has been unable to decide which one of us to give it to. Meg seems to feel (not that she told me this outright) that since Aunt March hasn't bestowed it on any of my sisters, she will give it to me this Christmas.

I should like to have something that none of my sisters was able to acquire. It is hardest being youngest and getting hand-me-downs all the time. Jo, of course, is the worst, but even Meg and Beth behave as though because I'm the youngest I cannot possibly know or understand things as well as they do.

If I do get the jewelry (a cameo brooch, if I've understood things correctly), I shall be very pleased, no matter how small or insignificant the piece of jewelry actually is.

I'm sure Meg and Jo and Beth all wrote wonderful Christmas letters full of the joy and spirit of the holiday. And here all I've done is discuss how truly awful it is to be youngest and how much I want to be given something none of my sisters have owned. Oh, well. I don't suppose anyone else will ever read this letter, and I know exactly how I feel, so I won't surprise myself.

How nice it would be to wear the cameo in front of my sisters. I wonder if Aunt March truly means to give it to me, and if she will do so this Christmas. I cannot imagine anything that would make me happier.

Amy March

CHAPTER 1

"Oh, Aunt March," said Amy, looking at the tiny cameo brooch her great-aunt had just handed her. "It's beautiful."

"It belonged to your great-grandmother," Aunt March said. "Your father's grandmother. It was given to her when she was ten years old."

"How happy she must have been to receive it," Amy said, gently closing the box the cameo came in and handing it back to Aunt March. "And what joy it must bring you to own it."

"The time has come for me to part with it," Aunt March said. "Over the years I have debated with myself which one of my grandnieces should own it next. I have decided upon one at last."

Amy smiled at Aunt March. "It could not have been an easy decision," she said.

"It wasn't," Aunt March said. "I thought I would give it to Meg. She is the oldest, after all. But there was a most unfortunate incident that forced me to change my mind."

Amy regretted having been too young at the time to have noticed an unfortunate incident. "I'm so sorry," she said. "Meg is a dear and deserves lovely things."

"Meg is entirely too much like her parents, I'm afraid," said Aunt March. "I had so hoped she would make a good marriage, but I suspect she'll marry for love, as your parents did, and be of no use to her sisters whatsoever."

Amy had every intention of marrying for love. She also had every intention of loving only a rich man. She looked at Aunt March and nodded sadly.

"Then I considered Josephine," said Aunt March. "Not for long, I admit, but I gave her her due. Still, we both knew it would be a dreadful mistake to give her anything so precious and delicate."

"Jo does make a mess of things," Amy said, touching the ink stain on her hand-me-down dress that years of washing had been unable to remove.

"Next it was Beth's turn," Aunt March said. "An unlikely choice, I grant you. But she really seemed to understand the significance of the brooch. And she asks for so little, I thought it might be a fine reward for her to receive it."

"Beth is very sweet," said Amy.

"Too sweet," said Aunt March. "She informed me that if she received the brooch she would never wear it herself but would pass it around for her sisters' benefit. If I had wanted her sisters to have it, I would have given it to one of them. So we agreed she was not the appropriate recipient."

"You must have been very disappointed," Amy said.

"I have been," said Aunt March. "But now I believe I have found just the right person." She smiled at Amy.

Amy smiled back. It wouldn't do to appear too eager, but it also wouldn't do to appear indifferent. "It is a beautiful brooch," she said.

"And all the more special for being a March family heirloom."

"Indeed," said Aunt March. "Amy, would you like it if I gave the brooch to you?"

"Oh, Aunt March!" cried Amy. "I should be so very grateful."

"Then it is yours," Aunt March said. "Cherish it, Amy, and keep it from harm so that one day you may give it to your daughter, and she may learn the story of how you received it from me."

Aunt March handed the box back to Amy, who made a big show of opening it again and staring at the cameo. It really was small. But it was nicely crafted, Amy noticed, and things of beauty gave her real pleasure.

"I can't get over its delicacy," she said to Aunt March. "A fine jeweler must have made it."

"I'm afraid I don't know its origin," Aunt March replied. "It's British, I believe, and your great-grandmother was ten when she received it. My husband knew nothing else about the piece. He was a fine man, but jewelry never interested him."

"I shall cherish it always," said Amy. "And I

139

shall cherish even more the fact that you chose me to give it to. Thank you, Aunt March."

"You're most welcome, my dear," said Aunt March. "You may give me a kiss if you wish."

Amy smiled and kissed her great-aunt on the cheek. "Might I wear the brooch now?" she asked. "I know I should save it for special occasions, but I do long to wear it."

"I think this is a special occasion," said Aunt March. She helped Amy pin the brooch to her dress. Amy ran to the mirror across the room and looked at the cameo. It hadn't gotten any bigger outside its box, but she loved the way it looked on her.

"I am the most fortunate girl in the world," she said. She could see Aunt March's smiling reflection in the mirror and whirled to show her how the cameo looked.

Aunt March cleared her throat. "As you know, I love all my nephew's daughters equally," she said. "But I do believe, Amy, there is a special bond between us."

"I feel it also," said Amy.

"I also am sure it will be you who makes the great society marriage," said Aunt March.

"But for that to happen, much needs to be done."

"I should love to marry well," said Amy, "so that I might help my family."

Aunt March looked straight at her.

Amy laughed. "And so that I could go to balls and wear beautiful gowns and have servants to do my bidding," she said.

Aunt March smiled, as Amy had suspected she would. "It is never too early to learn the social graces that will be required of a girl who wishes to make such a marriage," she said. "You are very pretty, Amy, and you have charm and intelligence. But although your family is a fine one, they have no money, and the well-to-do prefer to marry the well-to-do. If you are to overcome that handicap, it must be with my help."

"Oh, Aunt March," said Amy. "You are too good to me."

"It is for your family's benefit as well as your own," said Aunt March. "I was planning this Christmas to go to New York City and visit friends. A fine family, with two sons aged twelve and fourteen. Of course it's too early to think about marriage, but there would be no harm in their meeting you now. Would you care to make the trip with me?"

"To New York City?" Amy asked. "Oh, Aunt March. That's beyond my wildest dreams."

"Very well," Aunt March said. "I'm sure your parents won't object. You shall accompany me to New York next week."

"This is the happiest day of my life," Amy said, fingering the cameo. "Thank you, Aunt March, for all you have done for me." And this time, Amy kissed her great-aunt without being asked.

CHAPTER 2

"I'm not sure," Marmee said that night at supper. "I hate the idea of one of my daughters being away from home on Christmas. And of all of them, you, Amy, the youngest."

"But Marmee," Amy said. "I've never been to New York. I've never been anywhere. And I'll be with Aunt March."

"What fun that will be," said Jo. "I do believe I'd rather be in Hades without Aunt March than New York City with her."

"Jo," said Father.

"I'm sorry," Jo said. "I'm jealous. I should dearly love to go to New York, even if it did mean accompanying Aunt March as she makes her social calls."

"I should love those social calls," said Amy. "Father, Marmee, I might never have this chance again. Please say you'll let me go."

"You're ten years old," Marmee said. "You'll have many such chances. But how many Christmases with your family will you have?"

"I'm sure I'll appreciate them even more if I spend one Christmas away from home," Amy said. "Oh, Meg, tell Marmee and Father how important this is."

"I think they can see that," Meg said. "Marmee, I'll miss Amy at Christmastime too. But it is a wonderful opportunity for her."

"I think Amy should be allowed to go," said Beth. "When I went to New York City, I had a wonderful visit. And I know how much Amy wanted to go then. It wouldn't be fair that I should have such an experience and Amy not be allowed the same."

"But it won't be the same," said Marmee. "You went with your father and me, Bethy. We stayed at the home of friends. According to this note of Aunt March's, she and Amy will stay in a hotel."

"We will?" Amy asked. She hadn't known

that. A real hotel. The trip was becoming even more fabulous.

"And New York City is dangerous at Christmastime," Marmee said. "I've read articles in newspapers and magazines. There's a great deal of public drunkenness."

"I'm sure Aunt March will take great care to avoid bad neighborhoods," Father said. "It would be an opportunity for Amy to see New York City. I doubt I'll have the chance to take her there anytime soon."

"Let Amy go," Jo said. "She gets along well with Aunt March, and the two of them will have a fine time together."

Even Jo was on her side. Amy touched the cameo and felt a momentary flash of sorrow that she had been so greedy for the brooch. Her sisters were really wonderful, and if any of them ever wanted to borrow the cameo, she would be sure to lend it, just as long as Aunt March didn't know.

"Amy, is this so very important to you?" Marmee asked.

Amy nodded. She knew better than to tell Marmee that the true purpose of the visit was to start looking for a wealthy husband. "I know I'll miss you," she said, and she realized that was true. "But I'll be doing a good deed, keeping Aunt March company. And I should so love to see New York City."

Marmee sighed. "I wish I could keep my daughters with me forever," she said. "But I have to acknowledge they are all growing up. Very well, Amy. Have your Christmas adventure. But think of us on Christmas Day and know how much we'll be missing you."

Amy smiled. A trip to New York City was more than a Christmas adventure for her. It was a Christmas dream come true.

CHAPTER 3

Could there be a place more exciting than New York City?

Since she was a little child, Amy had dreamed of the great cities of Europe, with their magnificent cathedrals and castles and works of art. But New York City was like Amy herself, a youngest child, filled with energy and ambition and the determination to be the best.

There were people everywhere she looked — at the train station, on the streets, in front of the grand hotel Aunt March had selected for their stay. Some were dressed in coats of velvet and fur. Others wore more simple clothing, similar to the coat Amy herself had on. Still others were dressed in rags, with hardly any outer clothing to protect them from the December cold.

But no matter how they dressed, all these New Yorkers moved about as though they were in a mad rush to get somewhere. Even Aunt March, who had some difficulty walking, quickened her pace as she and Amy walked from their hansom cab to the hotel.

Amy would have liked to linger just a bit in the street, to have more of a chance to see the people, especially the fancily dressed ones. She would have enjoyed seeing the decorated storefronts as well, and the houses with their Christmas trees in the front parlor windows. But it was a cold day, and she sympathized with Aunt March's desire to be inside where it was warm.

As they rushed into the hotel, Amy caught sight of a girl standing by the door. She had on the flimsiest of dresses and a shawl that could not possibly have protected her from the brisk wind. In her hand were matches, which she offered mutely to the passersby. Few seemed to notice her, and even fewer stopped to make a purchase or simply give the child a penny.

Amy wanted to call Aunt March's attention

149

to the girl, perhaps to convince her to buy a bundle of matches, but Aunt March had her eyes only on the hotel door. Amy followed her aunt in, and once she saw the opulence of the hotel lobby, she forgot about the match girl standing outside.

It was the most splendid room Amy had ever seen, nearly the size of the March house, she estimated, and filled with heavy red velvet drapes and huge bronze planters filled with giant green ferns.

And the people in the lobby! Even the servants were dressed in spotless uniforms with crisp, clean white aprons. The guests wore the finest dresses and suits. Amy imagined herself in one such dress and shuddered with pleasure.

"You're cold too, I see," said Aunt March. "Very well. We'll warm up in our room and have dinner in the hotel tonight. Tomorrow we'll visit my friends the Cosgroves after church."

"Yes, Aunt March," Amy said. She was eager to see their room, and when she did, she wasn't disappointed. The room was large, warmed by a fire that gave off a special glow.

The windows overlooked the newly built Central Park, and Amy could see people skating on a pond that made her think of Walden Pond back home. For an instant she was homesick and pictured her family as they must be on Christmas Eve, wrapping presents and singing carols by the piano, which Beth played so prettily.

Why had she agreed to spend Christmas with Aunt March? she asked herself. But then she looked around the room and saw the paintings on the walls, the elaborate furnishings, the gaslights that made even the farthest corners bright and inviting, and she smiled. No matter how much she might miss her family and her home, this was going to be a Christmas she would never forget.

Dinner that night at the hotel restaurant was all Amy could have dreamed of. The grand room was decorated with garlands of pine and holly and satin ribbons, and a Christmas tree far more elaborately trimmed than any she had ever seen stood tall in the center. Aunt March was sure they'd be offered Christmas goose for dinner the next day, so she insisted that Amy and she have roast beef instead. Amy didn't care. Her family would be having a simple supper on Christmas Eve, and no matter how fine a cook Hannah was and how well the family ate on Christmas Day, she knew what she was being offered was a hundred times more expensive. Amy only wished she had finer clothing. Her dress was the simplest in the room. She was glad she had her cameo brooch, especially when Aunt March looked at the other hotel guests and said disapprovingly, "New money."

"Are the Cosgroves new money?" Amy asked Aunt March. She supposed she should know more about the boys she was to meet, especially if one of them might end up marrying her.

"Neither old nor new," said Aunt March. "I believe Mr. Cosgrove's grandfather made most of his money profiteering in the War of 1812. I went to school with Julia Bates, who later married George Cosgrove. We remained friends, and it is her son and his family we will be dining with tomorrow."

"Is your friend Mrs. Cosgrove still alive?" Meg asked.

"She is indeed, and she lives with her son,"

Aunt March replied. "While you make the acquaintance of the two Cosgrove lads, John and Richard, I shall visit with Julia. I believe there will be other guests as well. It should be quite a festive event."

"I look forward to it," Amy said, but in spite of herself, she yawned.

"I think what you most look forward to is a good night's sleep," said Aunt March. "And truth be told, so do I. After supper we'll go to our room and refresh ourselves for all that will happen tomorrow."

CHAPTER 4

As Amy and Aunt March left for church the next morning, Amy caught sight of the girl selling matches. A closer examination made Amy realize the girl was roughly her age. She was terribly thin, and she shivered as she extended her hand to try to entice people to buy her matches. Once again, though, Aunt March seemed oblivious to her. They hurried the two blocks to the church they would be attending.

The church was as ornate as the hotel, and Amy found herself missing the simple little church her father ministered. But this church had an organ that filled the space with the beauty of its sound, and the choir sang its celebration of Christmas in tones so perfect that

Amy wept with pleasure. The minister's sermon went on forever, giving Amy an opportunity to glance about and admire the clothing everyone wore. Father's sermons were far shorter and more pointed, but the clothing of even the best Concord ladies was nowhere near this splendid.

Amy and Aunt March didn't linger after the service. Instead they exchanged Christmas wishes with the people sitting in the pews nearest them, then left the church to walk to the Cosgrove home. Amy was glad it was a short walk, for the day was cold and blustery. She couldn't help thinking of the girl who sold matches and how cold she must be.

The Cosgrove home was filled with lights and Christmas wreaths and appetizing aromas. Aunt March was greeted like a long-lost relation, and Amy was much fussed over by Mrs. Cosgrove. Introductions were made all around, and Amy was brought to meet John and Richard. She looked at them carefully. They were good-looking boys, but both had sulky expressions.

"So you're Amy," Richard said. "Grandmama said we must be polite to you."

"I hope that won't be too great a burden," said Amy, thinking Richard quite the rudest boy she'd ever met.

"Christmas Day is such a bore," said John. "We opened our presents last night, and this morning we had to attend church, and now there's nothing left to do except eat our dinner and talk to strangers."

"Did you get nice presents?" Amy asked. She had not yet gotten any of hers, since Marmee had decided they should wait until she returned home.

John shrugged. "Clothes," he said. "Books. A cricket bat."

"Some toys," said Richard. "Games. Money."

"Those sound like wonderful presents," Amy said. "You must have enjoyed opening them last night."

"It was all right, I suppose," said John.

"I don't suppose you brought us something," said Richard.

"No," Amy said, wishing she were back home where the gifts were simple and inexpensive but selected and given with much love.

The boys fell silent. Amy looked around the parlor and tried to find something to converse about. "I've never been to New York before," she said. "It's all so splendid."

"It's all right, I suppose," John said again. "But nothing compared to Europe. I'll be taking the grand tour when I finish school."

"There are so many people in New York," Amy persisted. "I've never seen such fine ladies and gentlemen."

"New Yorkers pride themselves on their appearance," said Richard. "I suppose it's different where you come from."

It was, but Amy didn't care to admit it. "I saw many poor people as well," she said. "There was a girl no older than I am selling matches in front of our hotel."

"Little beggars," said John. "Such a bother."

"Guttersnipes," said Richard. "It's a crime they're allowed on our streets."

Amy decided it was time to change the subject, but she could find nothing else the Cosgrove boys cared to speak about. Instead they showed her their presents until it was time for Christmas dinner.

Aunt March had been right: They were served goose. There was food for twenty on the table, and only twelve to eat it. Amy had never seen such an abundance of leftovers. In spite of herself, she pictured the girl who sold matches and remembered how thin she was. But Amy didn't think Aunt March would approve if she asked for some food to take back to the hotel.

The afternoon droned on as endlessly as the sermon had that morning. Amy entertained herself by wandering around the house and admiring the furnishings. She made cheerful conversation with Julia Cosgrove and Aunt March and did all she could to show her pleasure and gratitude at spending the holiday with such a fine family. She tried to hide her boredom, and apparently succeeded, since Aunt March commended her manners as they walked back to the hotel.

But Amy hardly listened. She was waiting to see if the match girl was still there. Surely even she had a place to be on Christmas. But no, the girl stood outside the hotel door, holding out the matches, gratefully curtsying when anyone even looked her way.

"Come, Amy," said Aunt March. "I'm ready for a nap. Let's go to our room and rest awhile."

Amy followed Aunt March to their room. Aunt March's gentle snoring lulled her to sleep.

CHAPTER 5

The next thing Amy knew, she was shivering on the street. The wind was cutting through her, and when she looked down she saw she had no mittens on and her shoes had holes. No wonder she was so cold. Then she discovered that her coat was gone as well.

"What has happened?" she asked herself, but no one seemed to hear her. All around, people were madly rushing from place to place. No one cared that she was cold and hungry.

When did I eat last? she wondered. She couldn't remember ever being so hungry.

"Marmee!" she called. "Father!" But no one heard her. Suddenly she knew she was alone in the world. No one cared about her. She could die on the street and all those busy people would hardly even notice.

She found she had some matches in her hand. Perhaps she could sell them and make money for food that way. "Matches! Matches!" she cried, but her words were drowned out by the sounds of the people and the wind rushing by. Only the matches could keep her from dying, but no one bought any.

Two boys who looked familiar happened by. She realized they were John and Richard Cosgrove. Surely they would recognize her. "Please!" she called out to them. "Won't you buy some matches, please?"

"Filthy guttersnipe," Richard said, looking at her with disgust.

"I am not!" Amy shouted. "I'm Amy March. Do you hear me? I'm Amy March!"

But he didn't care. No one cared. Amy felt the tears pour down her cheeks. The matches wouldn't be enough to save her.

Amy sat bolt upright. She wiped the tears from her face. Where was she? What had happened? She discovered she was in bed, with Aunt March sleeping soundly by her side.

Looking around her, Amy remembered that she was in New York, sharing a magnificent hotel room with Aunt March. She was cold only because Aunt March had gathered the quilt over herself and the fire in their room had almost died out.

After dressing quietly, Amy left the room and made her way down to the lobby. Its air of wealth and luxury, which had so impressed her upon her arrival, did nothing to cheer her.

She pushed open the heavy glass front door and looked outside. Even at this late hour, the match girl was trying to make a few pennies. "Matches?" the girl asked her.

Amy walked over to her. "Here," she said, taking the cameo brooch off her dress and handing it to the match girl. "Take this."

The girl's eyes widened. "I couldn't possibly. Why would you even want to give that to me?"

"Because I have nothing else to give you," said Amy. "Take it. You can sell it someplace and get money for food and clothing."

The girl shook her head. "They'll think I stole it," she said. "I'll be arrested for sure."

"Wait here," Amy said. She ran back into the hotel lobby and went to the front desk. "Might I have some paper and a pen?" she asked.

"Certainly, miss," the man behind the desk replied. He gave her a lovely piece of hotel stationery and a fine pen.

Amy looked down at the paper, trying to decide just how to word her note. When she was finally satisfied, she began to write.

This cameo brooch belongs to me, Amy March. I've given it to this girl to sell because it's Christmas and she's hungry and cold. No one stole the cameo from me.

Amy March

Amy ran back outside. She wished she had thought to wear her coat, but as she looked at the match girl, she was glad she hadn't. Amy had never realized just how wealthy she was until she saw the match girl. If she'd had her coat with her, Amy would probably have given that to her as well.

"Take this note," Amy said.

164

"What's it say?" the girl asked.

"Can't you read?" Amy asked.

The girl shook her head.

"That's all the better," Amy said. "For then no one will suspect you wrote the note. It only says the brooch is mine to give and I've given it to you. Now you may take the brooch and sell it."

"Really?" the girl asked.

"Really," Amy said.

The girl began to cry. She grabbed Amy's hand and kissed it. "Thank you, miss," she said. "Thank you, thank you."

"That's perfectly all right," Amy said. "Now go and sell the brooch, and buy yourself a warm coat and some food."

"I will," the match girl said. "I'll never forget this, not for as long as I live. Bless you."

Amy watched as the girl ran down the street, clutching the cameo in her nearly frozen hand. Amy wondered as she walked back into the hotel what she could possibly tell Aunt March. Much to her sorrow, she found that only the truth would do.

"You did what?" Aunt March cried as Amy

tried to tell her the story over breakfast the next morning. "You gave the brooch to a street urchin?"

"I had to," Amy said. "I have so much, and she had nothing."

"You have very little yourself, my child," said Aunt March. "Your family is as poor as church mice."

"But we have clothes to keep us warm and food enough to eat," Amy said. "And she had nothing."

"You cannot save the world with impulsive acts of charity," said Aunt March. "The poor will always be with us."

"I know," Amy said. "And I know how important the brooch was to you, Aunt March. I wish I had something else I could have given her, but as you just pointed out, I don't have very much else."

Aunt March shook her head. "I had such hopes for you. Your parents have four daughters, and if none of you makes a good marriage, it will be ruination for your whole family. But I can see you are far more like your parents than I had thought. Good people, both of them, but with no sense of what is needed in this world. No sense at all."

"Yes, Aunt March," Amy said. She knew Aunt March did not approve of what she had done, and she knew that Aunt March had every right to be enraged at her. She knew, too, that the trip to New York was ruined. She knew all that, and yet she was glad she had given the brooch to someone in need.

CHAPTER 6

"You did what?" Jo asked as Amy sat by the fire and warmed herself the day after she returned from New York.

"I gave the brooch away," Amy said. "I'm sorry, Jo. I know the brooch belonged to you as much as it did to me. But you should have seen that girl. She was so thin, so cold."

Jo laughed. "I never cared about the brooch, you silly goose," she said. "I just can't get over the idea that you did such a thing."

"It was wonderful of you," Beth said. "I only wish I'd have the courage to do something like that, knowing how angry it would make Aunt March."

"How angry was she?" Meg asked.

"Angrier than I've ever seen her," Amy replied. "Of course, we don't have the sorts of rows she and Jo have. But she scarcely spoke to me the rest of the trip. Mostly she shook her head and said I would prove the ruination of the March family."

Jo laughed again. "It's nice to have that burden removed from my shoulders," she said. "Amy, what you did was absolutely capital."

"Don't use slang," Meg said. "But Jo's right, Amy. It was a fine thing you did."

"Have you told Father and Marmee yet?" Beth asked.

Amy shook her head. "Aunt March gave me a letter for them, but I thought I'd tell you the story first."

"I'm sure they'll understand," Beth said. "They're so generous themselves."

"I hope so," Amy said.

"Here they are now, just back from their walk," Jo said. "Do you want us with you when you tell them what happened?"

Amy shook her head. "I acted on my own," she said. "I might as well face them on my own."

"They'll understand," Meg said, giving Amy a kiss. She led Jo and Beth up the stairs to their bedrooms.

"What a wonderful day for a walk," Father said as he and Marmee entered the parlor. "What a shame none of you joined us, although I'm sure you enjoyed your reunion. Tell me, Amy, where are your sisters?"

"They went upstairs, Father," Amy said. "I asked them to. There's something I have to discuss with you, and I prefer to do it alone."

"What could that be?" Father asked, taking off his coat and helping Marmee with hers. "It sounds important."

"Here," Amy said, handing him Aunt March's letter. "I'm sure this will explain." She watched as Father opened the letter and he and Marmee read it together.

Marmee looked up first. "You gave away your great-grandmother's cameo?" she asked. "Oh, my."

"Just like that?" Father asked. "To a beggar girl on the street?"

"She wasn't a beggar," Amy said. "She sold matches. But yes, I suppose that is what I did. I just gave the brooch away."

"Did you ever see the girl again?" Marmee asked.

Amy shook her head. "She stood in front of the hotel until I gave her the brooch," she said. "But I didn't see her for the remainder of our stay. I suppose she sold the brooch and used the money for food and shelter for herself and her family. I don't know. I didn't really talk to her." Amy looked away from her parents. "The truth is I didn't want to know," she said. "I just couldn't stand the idea that she was so cold. I felt I had to do something, and all I could do was give her the brooch. I suppose if I were older, I could have found out where she lived and tried to help her family. But I didn't know how to do any of those things. And I'm not really sure I would have wanted to."

"It was my grandmother's brooch," Father said. "I have very little of my grandparents'. A book or two. A lock of my grandmother's hair. Not much besides that."

"I know," Amy said. "I'm sorry."

Father smiled. "You have nothing to be sorry about. My grandparents weren't the sort of people who insisted on holding on to things. I didn't know my grandmother well, but I'm certain she'd be pleased with what you did."

"More pleased than Aunt March, anyway," said Marmee.

"I angered her, I know," said Amy.

Father raised his eyebrows. "Sometimes," he said, "just sometimes, mind you, Aunt March is wrong. In my opinion, this is one of those times. Come here, Amy, and let me show you with a kiss just how proud I am of you."

Amy walked to her father and felt herself enveloped in his arms. As long as she had his love, she knew, she would never be hungry and she would never be cold. And the sweetness of that moment meant more to her than a hundred trips to New York or a thousand cameo brooches.

PORTRAITS OF
LITTLE WOMEN
ACTIVITIES

DRIED FRUIT LOAF

Dried fruits add a colorful accent to baked goods, as you'll see when you cut into this deliciously moist loaf.

INGREDIENTS
- 1 cup dried figs
- 1 cup golden raisins
- 1 cup dried cherries or cranberries
- 1½ cups water
- 1 cup pitted dates
- ¼ cup solid shortening
- ¾ cup sugar
- 1 egg
- 1 teaspoon grated orange zest
- 2 cups flour
- 2 teaspoons baking powder
- 1 teaspoon baking soda
- 1 teaspoon salt

Preheat oven to 350 degrees. Grease two
9-by-5-inch loaf pans.

1. Place figs, golden raisins, and dried
   cherries in small pan and add water.
   Simmer over low heat for 5 minutes.
   Drain, reserving ⅔ cup of the liquid.
   Let the fruit cool, then chop it with the
   dates.
2. Put shortening in a bowl and add sugar,
   egg, and orange zest. Beat until creamy.
3. In another bowl, mix the flour, baking
   powder, baking soda, and salt with a
   fork.
4. Add the dry ingredients to the shortening mixture and stir just until combined.
5. Add the fruit, stir in the reserved fruit
   liquid, and blend well.
6. Spoon the batter into the pans and let
   them stand 15 minutes.
7. Bake about 45 minutes, or until a straw
   comes out clean.

These dried fruit loaves make great holiday
gifts. Just wrap each one in heavy-duty
aluminum foil and tie with a colorful bow.

CHRISTMAS SUGAR COOKIES

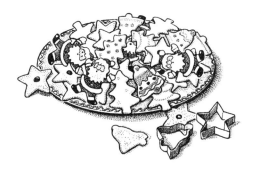

Warm from the oven, these delicious cookies in the shapes of bells, Christmas trees, stars, and Santas are lovely arranged on a pretty plate—and are scrumptious to eat.

INGREDIENTS

 1½ cups sifted all-purpose flour
 ¾ cup sugar
 ½ teaspoon baking powder
 ½ teaspoon salt
 ½ teaspoon baking soda
 ½ cup butter
 1 large egg
 2 teaspoons milk
 1 teaspoon vanilla

Preheat oven to 375 degrees. Grease a cookie sheet.

1. In a bowl, sift together flour, sugar, baking powder, salt, and baking soda.
2. Cut the butter into the flour mixture and work in with your fingers until mixture looks like coarse cornmeal.
3. Add egg, milk, and vanilla.
4. Roll dough out on well-floured surface to desired thickness (⅛ inch or a bit thicker).
5. Cut using holiday cutters and place on greased cookie sheet.
6. Bake for 8 minutes.
7. *Optional*: To decorate with colored sugar, sprinkle sugar onto desired areas before baking. To decorate with icing, bake cookies, allow to cool, and ice.

Decorated or plain, these holiday sugar cookies add a festive touch to any dessert tray.

Makes about 3 dozen cookies, depending on the size of the cutters.

CHRISTMAS ANGEL DOLL

Constructed from a wooden clothespin, this little doll makes a lovely Christmas tree decoration, adds a special touch to gift wrappings, and is a perfect gift by itself. It's fun and easy to put together.

MATERIALS

1 round-top wooden clothespin
1 white and 1 gold pipe cleaner
1 yard beige, brown, black, or yellow yarn for hair
¼ yard white or off-white tulle, satin, or other soft fabric

1 yard of ½-inch-wide white sheer or satin ribbon

1 bottle all-purpose, nontoxic, clear-drying craft glue

1 spool white thread

1 needle

1 fine paintbrush (if using craft paint)

1 small bottle fine gold, silver, or crystal glitter

Scissors

Hair spray

Craft paint: beige or brown for angel's face, red, and black. If you don't have paint, use marker pens.

ASSEMBLY

Note: Putting the split end of the clothespin over the rim of a glass will steady the pin for painting.

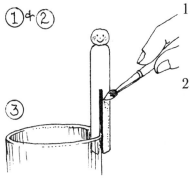

1. Paint or color round top of clothespin with beige or brown. Allow to dry.
2. Paint face onto round top: two small black dots for the eyes, one small black dot for the nose, a small red semicircle

stitch...

...pull

(curving up) for the mouth, and two small red dots for the cheeks. Allow to dry.

3. Paint the rest of the clothespin white and allow to dry.

4. Fold tulle, or other fabric, into a strip 4 inches wide and 14 inches long. Sew a running stitch along top end of fabric and gather material by pulling on thread from the needle end. Fit material around doll's waist and sew in place. Make sure skirt fits snugly and doesn't slip. (Put a dab of glue at back of seam before you sew skirt in place to secure it.)

5. Cut lengths of yarn, about 1¹/₄ inch

long, then place dab of glue at center of each piece of yarn and fasten to top of clothespin. Repeat until head is covered with enough "hair." If hair looks too long or raggedy, even off ends with scissors.

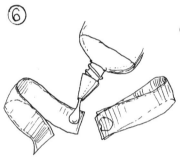

6. Cut two lengths of white ribbon about 2 ¼ inches long for the wings. Fold one length over to make a loop. Put dab of glue at cut end and press two ends together. Allow to dry. Repeat with second length of ribbon.

7. Take one loop, place cut ends at back of angel's waist, and glue into place. Take second loop and repeat. Allow

loops to spread out at sides of angel's head to be seen from front.

8. For angel's halo, take a length of gold pipe cleaner about 2 inches long. Make a small circle and secure end to remaining length of pipe cleaner. Secure loop by twisting it onto stem or gluing it. Place dab of glue at end of stem, which should be about 1 inch long, and glue it to back of angel's head, allowing halo to rest on hair.

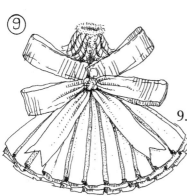

9. Take another length of white ribbon and tie around angel's waist, making a bow and letting streamers

hang down back of skirt.

10. For angel's arms, cut two lengths of white pipe cleaner, each about 2 inches long, and glue one end of each strip. Place on either side of angel.

11. Lay a piece of newspaper on a flat surface, spray skirt and hair with hair spray, and sprinkle with glitter. Allow to dry and gently shake off excess glitter.

Wherever you display it, your beautiful angel doll will add sparkle and grace.